'What is it with you?' A̶ ̶a̶l̶r̶e̶a̶d̶y̶ ̶s̶a̶i̶d̶.

Claire was totally unready for this kind of confrontation with him. Her own thoughts were still whirling around in her head; she needed to sort them out, marshal them into order, before she attempted to cross swords with him.

'I don't know what you mean,' she said icily.

'You know well enough. There's something about me that makes you uncomfortable. You think I'm crazy. You don't approve of my methods, you distrust my motives. All right. You don't have to like me—nor I, you—that isn't part of the deal, but both of us have a job to do. So get off my back, and let's get on with it.'

'The only thing about you that makes me uncomfortable is that you've done your best to embarrass and wrong-foot me from the moment we met!' she exploded furiously.

'Then you're easily embarrassed, lady! What I need is a fair-minded journalist who'll give a straight, unbiased report on my work, not a pampered female who gets the vapours if a man looks at her, and is repelled by the thought of a little hard work!'

HAZARDOUS ASSIGNMENT

BY
LEE STAFFORD

MILLS & BOON LIMITED
ETON HOUSE   18-24 PARADISE ROAD
RICHMOND   SURREY   TW9 1SR

First published in Great Britain 1989
by Mills & Boon Limited

© Lee Stafford 1989

Australian copyright 1989
Philippine copyright 1989
This edition 1989

ISBN 0 263 76305 6

Set in Times Roman 10 on 11½ pt.
0-8905-56320 C

Made and printed in Great Britain

CHAPTER ONE

BEFORE her arrival in Rio Negro three days earlier, Claire Mallory would have scoffed at the idea that she could have so much difficulty with a small transaction like ordering some bottled water to be sent up to her colleague's room. She was sure that her Spanish, although rudimentary, was up to this task, and that she had not mispronounced anything. She could also have sworn that the clerk on the desk was determined *not* to understand her.

Fighting against weariness and irritability, and a strong temptation to lose her temper, it suddenly occurred to her that she was going about things the wrong way. If Ashley Wade were already in the hotel, surely he could sort this out for her? First of all she needed to locate Dr Wade.

Claire swallowed, took a deep breath and began again.

'Está el Señor Wade aquí?' she enquired carefully. *'El doctor inglés.'*

The clerk heaved a sigh of relief, as if at last he had found a way to get this crazy foreign woman off his back.

'Sí,' he assured her earnestly.

'Donde está...' Claire began hopefully, and in reply he raised a languid arm and pointed vaguely over her shoulder.

Claire gasped as she turned and caught sight of the man who had entered the hotel lobby and was even now approaching the desk. He resembled some half-wild creature who had long since shunned civilisation—an explorer back from the Amazon jungle, a trapper returned from the Yukon. His trousers and jacket, which looked like some kind of ancient ex-Army battledress, were both shabby and filthy, his boots were mud-caked, and no part of him would appear to have been washed for a week. His hair was wild and dark, and his face was covered with a shaggy, unkempt growth of beard. He was an apparition, fearsome and disturbing. Claire was sure there must be some mistake. She had never met an Englishman who looked like this, and found it hard to envisage one entering an hotel in such a dishevelled and dirty condition.

She looked sharply at the clerk. Was he trying to send her up? Forgetting her efforts to communicate in Spanish, she said crisply, 'Excuse me, but that cannot be Dr Wade.'

The wild man had reached the desk and, horrified, Claire saw that from behind the facial stubble a pair of snapping blue, very un-Latin eyes regarded her with something oddly like amusement.

'I hate to tell you, lass,' he said, and there was a half-buried echo of Yorkshire in his voice, 'but I'm afraid it is.' He held out his hand, then dropped it. 'No, perhaps not. It's no cleaner than the rest of me. In fact, it would be better if I didn't come any closer. To put it frankly, I stink.' Very white teeth gleamed out from the bearded jaw. 'Miss Mallory, I presume?'

Claire was rarely at a loss for words, but this meeting was to her every bit as bizarre as Livingstone finding Stanley in the equatorial jungles of Africa. She had travelled all the way from England at the instigation of her editor for whom she wrote a regular medical column, accompanied by a top-flight photographer who was now snoring off the effects of *aguardiente* upstairs, and an executive of a multi-national manufacturing combine who was laid low with a stomach bug. Here she was, virtually alone in a seedy Central American hotel, with an unhelpful desk clerk and this...this madman! And what in London had looked like an exciting if slightly risky assignment had begun to take on the less amusing aspects of a comic opera.

The trail which had led her into this curious situation had begun quite innocently in London a few weeks earlier, with a routine call from Harold Jones, editor of *World Focus* magazine, to present herself in his office.

'Got a good one for you this time, Claire,' he said, as his secretary placed cups of coffee on the desk in front of them. 'Ever been to Latin America?'

'Good lord, no,' she said with a start. 'Never been further west than Dublin.'

'Well then, here's your chance. I want you to get yourself jabbed and visa'd and be ready to fly out to Rio Negro.'

'You're joking!' She stared at him doubtfully.

'I'm deadly serious.' In turn he regarded her speculatively, weighing up pros and cons. 'In a way, it's a disadvantage, your being a woman. Conditions will probably be dreadful. On the other hand, perhaps you can report from a more...shall we say, compassionate angle. Give it everything, Claire. This could be a big one, and *World Focus* has an exclusive on it. You'll be the only journalist involved.'

After she had recovered from her initial stupefaction, he had outlined the situation to her more fully.

'Rio Negro, in case you don't know, is a poverty-stricken Central American republic. You know the sort of place...constant political upheavals, a series of military dictators and a ruling clique who don't give two hoots for the needs of the populace at large. Two years ago, to add insult to injury, there was a horrendous earthquake—eight on the Richter scale, causing wholesale destruction over a large area.'

'I remember it.' Claire nodded. 'I thought at the time how unfair it seemed that the countries which suffer these great natural disasters are always the poorest and least stable. Go on.'

'An English GP just happened to be there at the time,' Harold continued. 'Purest coincidence—he was on a stopover on his way back from a trip to Australia. He found himself helping with the rescue work—first aid, emergency surgery—you know?'

'Not an unexpected thing for a doctor to do,' Claire observed. A GP's daughter herself, she knew that a doctor was always a doctor first and foremost. How could he fail to offer his services in a situation of such urgent and tragic need?

'Quite so. But this one didn't come home to England when the immediate crisis was over. He stayed on, ventured into the interior of the country, and found a neglected peasant population, poor and undernourished and without any kind of medical care. He was so affected by their plight that he decided the only solution was for him to provide that care.'

'Very laudable,' Claire remarked. 'So he's exchanged a job here for, admittedly, a more difficult one over there. What's newsworthy about that?'

'What's newsworthy, Claire, is that nobody is paying this man's salary. The Rio Negro government refuses to admit the need for a doctor in the area. In fact he's rather a thorn in their side, and he feels they would be glad to be rid of him. He runs his practice, which serves a vast area, on whatever he can scrounge and cajole from charity. After two years of this kind of existence, things were beginning to look grim, so he decided to tap the big boys. Like General Chemicals, who, among other things, own a pharmaceutical supplies company. It was they who got in touch with me.'

'A good move. General Chemicals sponsor medical research quite a lot,' she said. 'I interviewed someone from their Special Projects Department when I did that cancer research piece.'

'They were mightily impressed by that—and by the follow-up you wrote on chemotherapy,' he told her. 'Now they're planning to send someone from their organisation out to Rio Negro to see exactly what this man, Ashley Wade, is doing.'

'With a view to helping him?'

'If his work is as worthwhile as it sounds. They want a good journalist who specialises in medical matters to go with their representative.' He smiled. 'Don't let it go to your head, but they particularly wanted you.'

Claire was gripping the edge of her seat. Don't let it go to your head, he had warned, but that head was spinning with excitement and the glowing satisfaction of praise for her work. She was already wriggling with impatience, eager to get busy researching all she could find out about Rio Negro.

Harold noted her anxiety to be off. It was a good sign, and meant she was ticking over, but he had to put a brief curb on her enthusiasm.

'Before you start rushing around digging up info, I want you to meet Greg Telford, the man from General Chemicals with whom you will be going to Rio Negro. I hope you and he will get on, since we all stand to gain from this collaboration. *World Focus* gets a good, exclusive, topical piece of reportage, General Chemicals gets some favourable publicity—and Ashley Wade, hopefully, gets funding for his work.'

'It sounds as if he deserves it,' Claire said. She was already carrying in her head the image of a latter-day

Albert Schweitzer, a gentle soul, probably white-haired and elderly, dispensing care and comfort to the poverty-stricken peasantry of Rio Negro.

But when she met Greg Telford for a working lunch and saw the letter he had received from Ashley Wade, her benign vision was rudely jolted. The elderly saint of her imagination would write words to the effect of,

> Dear Sirs, I earnestly request your esteemed company to help me in my worthy endeavour...

Or something like that. Dr Wade began abruptly,

> This is a begging letter, so I won't dissemble. What I want from you is money, and with profits like yours, you should be able to spare a little...

Claire choked over her tomato and mozzarella starter. 'A bit curt, isn't he? That's not a begging letter. It's a demand for money with menaces!'

'Well, it certainly succeeded in grabbing our attention,' he said. 'After an opening sentence like that, one has to read on. And he then goes on to describe the conditions in which he works very clearly and with great impact. If only half of it is true, he deserves some recognition. Of course, we have to check it out, look into it first hand, and if we do decide to sponsor his efforts, sit down with him and discuss in detail how it can best be acheived. That's where I come in. And you, as the one most qualified to write an account of it.'

Greg Telford smiled. He was slim and elegant, beautifully turned out in a beige linen suit and ivory silk shirt, his hair brushed and trimly shaped to his head so that it appeared to have been sculpted into place.

'I don't imagine it's going to be too great a hardship working with you, Claire. I may call you Claire?' He placed his neatly manicured hand over hers. 'I asked for a journalist who specialised in medical reporting, but to be assigned one so attractive into the bargain is an unexpected bonus.'

Claire sipped her wine and retrieved her hand deftly. She was not unaware of the appreciative way he had been eyeing her throughout lunch, and decided to put an end to this line before he got properly launched on it.

'That's very kind of you, Mr Telford...Greg...but without reading too much into a casual compliment, I ought to point out that I'm an attached lady,' she said. Noticing his deliberate glance at her hands, she laughed. 'No, I didn't say I was married. Just part of a...a committed relationship.'

'You can't win them all,' he said, with a shrug. 'I could say, out of sight, out of mind, but if it's a serious involvement...?'

To equivocate here would be to hold out hope, so Claire said swiftly and definitely, 'It's serious enough. Let's get back to Dr Ashley Wade, shall we?'

He appeared to accept the put-down with reasonable grace, and Claire relaxed, although she admitted that describing herself as 'attached' was overstating the case. Jon had come into her life a few months earlier. He stayed at her flat as often as she would allow him to, ate her food, drank her Scotch, and littered her usually tidy domain with his discarded shirts, papers, and assorted rubbish. Periodically she decided she had had enough of this and showed him the door, as she had done last night, when she had come home late after a really draining day and found him ensconced there with half a dozen of his advertising agency cronies, the air thick with smoke, empty glasses and bottles everywhere—and a girl actually washing her hair in Claire's bathroom!

Maybe he would come back, maybe he wouldn't. He usually did, but this time she had been too tired and annoyed to be diplomatic about ejecting him, and she had made him lose face in front of his friends. Nor was she sure that she wanted him back. The trip to Central America was a good way of ensuring they had a break from one another, and, if she felt the same way on her return, the break might well be permanent.

But the last thing she needed right now was a flirtation with another man, and since she would have to travel with Greg Telford and spend a lot of time in his company, under who knew what strange circumstances, it was as well to make it clear from the start that she was not available. If what she had told him was a lie, she reassured herself it was only a white one.

So she had effectively neutralised Greg. And there would be no problems with Basil, the photographer. He had been living with Jane, his long-suffering girlfriend, for ages, and *her* only rival came out of a bottle. Claire put men out of her mind, had all the necessary injections, did her homework and bought some clothes suitable for rough travel in a hot climate. Then she closed up her flat and set off for Rio Negro.

But almost at once she began to have serious doubts about the assignment and her own ability to fulfil it. The ten-hour flight had been hell on wings to one whose knuckles were always white with terror the moment the wheels of the aircraft parted company with the runway. She had been relieved to arrive in one piece, but the brief sojourn in the country's capital had been utterly depressing. Parts of the city centre still resembled a bombed out war zone, giving the impression that little had been done to rebuild after the earthquake. A sleazy heat, made harder to bear by the humidity, had made her permanently lethargic, and the grinding poverty she saw all around her, the smell of decay rising like a miasma from the river after which the early explorers had named the country, filled her with a sense of hopelessness. If the rest were anything like this, Dr Ashley Wade was wasting his time—and so, presumably, was she.

After a day's rest, she felt a little better and her determination to do her job triumphed over her misgivings. The three of them rose early, before it was even light, to catch the bus to Aguas Calientes, a small town in the interior where they were to meet up with Dr Wade.

The bus was late. Not just minutes late, but more than an hour. No one in the patient queue waiting to board it seemed surprised by this. They all wore expressions of resignation, indicating that this was normal, and the man in the ticket office only shrugged his shoulders and feigned not to understand their queries.

'Man, this must be the original banana republic,' moaned Basil in the mid-Atlantic drawl he had affected after several years spent working in New York. He looked green around the gills, and was nursing a hangover. Not surprisingly, Claire thought, since he had been drinking steadily since they had left Heathrow. Still, she had worked with him before, and knew what to expect as soon as Harold informed her that 'Boozy Basil' would be her partner on this enterprise. Only the fact that he regularly turned out pictures of such stunning impact made any reputable journalist prepared to risk the hazards of working with him.

At last the bus—an antiquated boneshaker—arrived, and they quickly claimed their seats. The vehicle was full to capacity, the central aisle crammed with standing passengers. Old men nodded off stoically the minute they sat down, and in the seat next to Claire, a young woman unconcernedly suckled a baby. Already the air was hot, and the bus full of rank odours. Greg Telford's nose wrinkled fastidiously, and Claire suppressed a wry grin.

Then the torture began. The road was only tarmacked for a few miles outside the city, and after that it degenerated rapidly. The bus jolted and rattled ceaselessly until Claire was sure that every bone in her body was about to become disconnected. Yet, despite her discomfort, she could not fail to be awed by the scenery outside her window.

Leaving behind the cultivated rice and banana plantations, and passing through a belt of dense jungle, the road climbed through wild hill country with a horizon of misty blue mountains drawing ever closer. Apart from a few poor farms and tiny villages, the land appeared empty, and these vast, unpeopled distances were unnerving to the girl used to the bustle and the constant crowds of London. They wound on, through savagely beautiful gorges with sheer drops of several thousand feet alarmingly close to the bus wheels, where there was nothing to be done but close one's eyes and pray the driver knew his business.

Behind her, Basil snored gently; anaesthetised by the remains of a bottle of whisky, he slept through all the jarring and shaking. The sun rose higher in a blazing sky, and she felt disgustingly sticky from the heat, dust and perspiration. When would it end? Why had she ever agreed to undertake this job in the first place?

It was late afternoon before they trundled down through hills planted with coffee into the old colonial town of Aguas Calientes. The name indicated the presence of hot springs somewhere in the vicinity, but all Claire wanted was a cold shower, and the three of them stumbled wearily into the Hotel Principal in the main square of the town, too exhausted to take much notice of their surroundings.

'I've stayed in better hotels,' Greg muttered *sotto voce* in Claire's ear as the sleepy desk clerk checked their reservations.

She was past caring that the plaster was peeling off the walls in places, and the reception area had a run-down somnolence which suggested it was years since anyone had actually stayed there.

'The guide-book says it's the best in town,' she shrugged, accepting her key and smiling at the clerk, who stared stonily back at her. 'Besides, Dr Wade is due to meet us here tonight, so we may as well make the best of it. It's only for one night.'

He raised an elegant eyebrow.

'I'm supposed to be reassured by that? Tomorrow, who knows what delights await us, as we follow the intrepid doctor into yet more primitive parts,' he murmured. 'I'm beginning to wish that General Chemicals, in its infinite wisdom, had chosen someone else for this prestigious mission.'

'Where's the bar?' Basil interrupted laconically.

Claire pointed him gently towards the stairs.

'I'm sure there is one, but you ought to go to your room and have a rest first,' she suggested tactfully.

'Been sleeping on the bus all day, man,' he said, with the beginnings of truculence. 'I sure don't need any more rest—I need a drink.'

'He'll never make the journey tomorrow if he has too thick a head,' Greg observed as Basil disappeared in search of the bar. 'Besides, won't you need him sober enough to take photographs?'

'Not tonight, I shouldn't think.' Claire managed a smile. 'I assume we'll just be meeting Dr Wade and having dinner. Don't worry too much about the pics. I guarantee they'll be tremendous. Basil will do himself a mischief one day if he doesn't quit drinking, but you can always rely on the shots.'

'I sincerely hope you're right, or the board will have my hide,' he said aggrievedly.

Claire's bedroom looked out on the square, and she had a quick impression of graceful Spanish arches running along three sides of it, and a splendid baroque church dominating the fourth. The walls of the buildings were not white now but mellow ivory as the sun began to lose some of its power, and trees gave shady splashes of green to the picture. Beyond the rooftops the encircling hills darkened a little, cradling the town in a protective embrace. Why, it's beautiful, she thought, surprised, and began to feel more buoyant.

Minutes later, her brief rapport with Central America was ruined by her irritation with the shortcomings of the hotel. She had a wardrobe with only one coat-hanger, and a door which refused to stay shut. Well, it was scarcely worth unpacking for one night, and she could live with the creaking door. What she found more difficult to accept was that when she turned on the shower, no water came out.

Wrapped in a cotton bathrobe, Claire sat on the bed, picked up the phone and called the desk, explaining carefully that there wasn't any water.

'Sí, agua!' The comatose clerk who had given them their keys insisted that there was, and followed this with a spate of words Claire had no hope of understanding.

She gave up and tried the washbasin. Here, the stiff, rusty tap yielded a trickle of a few inches into the basin. With difficulty she sponged herself, removing, she was sure, only the top layer of accumulated grime. Cleaning her face with skin tonic, she put on a clean, if crumpled, skirt and top, and brushed her long, honey-blonde hair vigorously before twisting it in a knot on top of her head.

She sprayed herself vigorously with cologne in an attempt to make herself feel cleaner, and spared time for a quick, critical glance at her reflection. There was no rule which said that journalists, particularly female ones, had to look good, but in her opinion it couldn't harm.

Now for the mysterious Dr Ashley Wade! With a leap of excitement and curiosity, Claire wondered if the man they had travelled so far to meet had arrived yet. He might well have checked in before them and be already waiting.

The telephone rang abruptly, interrupting her thoughts, and she picked up the receiver.

'Claire? It's Greg.' He sounded plaintive and agonised. 'You and Basil will have to meet Dr Wade without me. I've got galloping gut-rot, or something, and I daren't stir too far from the bathroom! I was fine when we arrived—how can these things strike so quickly?'

'It's most likely the heat, or something you ate,' Claire said sympathetically. 'Certainly, you can't go out for a meal in that state. In fact, you shouldn't eat at all. Take a couple of those tablets we were given for stomach problems, and I'll have some bottled water sent up for you. You should drink as much fluid as possible.'

'You're a brick. Is it writing medical columns that gives you so much knowledge of these matters?'

'More likely, it's being a doctor's daughter,' Claire said in a practical tone. 'Don't worry, Greg. I'll make your apologies to Dr Wade. I'm sure he'll understand.'

But he had already rung off, abruptly. Claire sighed. It was, perhaps, inevitable that one of them should come down with some bug during their visit, in spite of all the precautions they had taken, but she hadn't expected it quite so soon, in the relative comfort of a town hotel. She went along the corridor to Basil's room, and, without much hope of a reply, tapped on the door.

There was no sound, so she opened it tentatively. Basil was indeed present, but he was flat out on his stomach, snoring sonorously. On the table beside him was a half-empty bottle of the fiery local spirit.

She shook him, gently at first, then more urgently.

'Basil—come on! Stop playing silly devils! We've got to meet Dr Wade.'

He merely turned over and lapsed back into heavy sleep. It was going to be several hours before he was even conscious, let alone ready to meet anyone. 'And then there was one,' Claire thought resignedly as she closed the door and went downstairs, leaving him to his stupor and his dreams.

CHAPTER TWO

DR ASHLEY WADE, if this were indeed he, did not give Claire the chance to discover much more on this initial meeting.

'There's no need to stare at me as if you were the Ancient Mariner,' he said with unexpected brusqueness. 'I simply thought I had better check that you'd arrived safely. I'd reckoned on being here before you, but it took longer than I'd expected. I'll go and render myself a bit more savoury, then I'll meet you all here in...' he paused '...say, an hour?'

'I'm afraid there's only me,' Claire said quickly. 'Mr Telford has unfortunately come down with a stomach bug, and Basil Firth... well, he's not feeling too good, either,' she finished lamely.

He did not, she thought, display an excess of sympathy for the sufferers.

'It's a fact of life, I'm afraid, that anywhere south of the Rio Grande that sort of attack is extremely common. Montezuma's revenge, the Aztec quickstep, whatever you choose to call it. If he has any remedy for it, he should take it, and drink plenty of fluids—the bottled kind.'

'I already told him that,' she said. 'I was trying to order some water when you arrived, but I can't get through to the clerk what I want. I must say, this place is badly named. You can't get water at any price—either to drink or to shower with.'

He shrugged, and looked at her with mild scorn. She flushed, aware of having sounded petulant and patron-

19

ising, the typical Anglo-Saxon traveller abroad, sulking over the lack of home comforts.

'That's Rio Negro for you,' he told her casually. 'It's either a feast or a famine where water is concerned. You'll find that at some times of the day it will run, at others, it won't. There's little point in complaining to the hotel—so far as they are concerned, the showers are in working order.'

He turned to the clerk and spoke swiftly in Spanish. *His* request was dealt with without too much resistance, Claire noted.

'He'll have some water sent up to your colleague right away. Don't interpret that too literally—it means in perhaps half an hour. If he hasn't recovered by tomorrow, I'll have a look at him, but my guess is that it will have passed by then. Now, then—what's up with the photographer?''

Claire did not care too greatly for his abrupt manner, and feared he would be even less sympathetic towards Basil's self-induced problem.

'He's...he'll be OK in the morning,' she said evasively.

Dr Wade gave a snort of amused understanding.

'I get it. He's been tasting the local spirit and is feeling no pain?' he suggested. 'My God, what a trek this promises to be—one member recovering from the trots, and another nursing a sore head! Are you quite sure you're fit and well, Miss Mallory?'

'I am in perfect health, Dr Wade, so you needn't trouble yourself about me,' she retorted sharply.

'I've other things to trouble myself with, lass,' he told her. 'I'll see you in an hour. Oh...and I suggest you don't wait for me in the hotel bar, alone. In Latin America, that will almost certainly be construed as an invitation.'

She was irritated by his warning. As if she were innocent or foolish enough to sit alone in a bar in a strange
city, on a continent which had invented the concept of
machismo. But as he turned towards the door she felt,
unreasonably, as though she were being abandoned.

'Aren't you...aren't you staying here?' she called after
him.

He grinned back rakishly beneath the beard.

'Nay, lass! This joint's too pricey for me,' he replied,
and disappeared out into the square.

Claire scratched her head, puzzled and thoughtful. The
Hotel Principal, for all it was the best in town, was by
no means luxurious, and could not be called expensive.
But the odd doctor was staying somewhere even cheaper,
and she dreaded to think what flea-pit of an estab-
lishment that must be. Was he simply trying to make
the point that he did not waste money on accommodation, or was he really that hard up? He was an enigma,
no doubt about it.

She shrugged and, going back upstairs, called to see
how Greg was feeling.

'Go away, Claire,' he insisted petulantly from the other
side of the door. 'This is not a condition in which any
man wants a woman to see him! Even if she *is* a medical
writer and a doctor's daughter!'

'All right, I'm on my way. I only wanted to let you
know that I have just made the brief acquaintance of
Dr Wade.'

'How did you find him?'

'Strange.' She hesitated. 'I'll say no more, and let you
form your own opinion. I'm meeting him again in an
hour, hopefully for dinner—oops! Sorry, Greg,' she
apologised, recalling the state of his stomach. 'I shouldn't
have mentioned that word. They're sending up some

bottles of water for you. Don't drink the stuff out of the taps, or you'll have something even worse.'

She returned to her room and tried to pass the time polishing up the notes she had already written as an introduction to her article, but the tone of them sounded so jaundiced and uncomplimentary about all she had so far seen in Rio Negro, she decided it would be fairer to leave them a while, in the hope that time might mellow her initial impressions.

It was dark now outside her window, and lights had come on in the square. The church was now just a shadowy hulk, and she thought of similar squares she had seen in Spain, and other European countries, where such a building would have been attractively floodlit to emphasise its beauty by night. With care, Aguas Calientes could be a place tourists might come to see, bringing in much-needed foreign currency. Did no one have the money to spend on making it so... or did no one care?

She had thought that all the reading and research she had done would have prepared her for what she would find here. But how could one who had lived all her life in a secure, temperate environment ever be fully prepared for the reality of Latin America? The debilitating heat, the dust, and the innumerable flying, creeping and crawling forms of life. The dirt and squalor and deprivation such as she had never encountered before. The blazing sun, the colour and noise, the dark faces and dark eyes of the people, emphasising the alien quality of her own almost Nordic fairness. The ever-present sense of a volatile imbalance that might, at any moment, tip over into chaos. And always, the incredible natural beauty of brilliant skies, vast horizons, and savage mountains, that caught one's breath with a physical force. It was more than Claire could take in all at once.

No wonder she felt disorientated and more than a little uneasy. And, with both her companions temporarily out of action, she was obliged to take the reins in her own hands. She had consoled herself with the knowledge that Ashley Wade was an Englishman and a doctor. Both of these qualifications would appear to endow him with a certain solidity and respectability, in spite of the rather rude introduction to his letter to General Chemicals.

But she was no more prepared for the reality of Ashley Wade than she had been for that of South America. Was he really what he professed to be, or was he a maniac, or some kind of conman? Had they all come out to Rio Negro on a wild-goose chase, with nothing at the end of it but disappointment—or worse? And where did she go from here?

The hour passed very slowly, but at last the appointed time arrived and, suppressing her apprehension, Claire went back downstairs to the lobby. But there was no sign of Dr Wade. Apart from the half-asleep clerk, who was yawning widely and gazing into space, there was only a man leaning on the far end of the reception desk, leafing idly through the pages of a newspaper. Her nervousness turned to worry of another kind. Had he really abandoned her, and taken off back into the wilds whence he came?

'Here you are, then,' an unmistakable voice said in English in her ear. 'A punctual female, of all things!'

It *was* Ashley Wade—or at least, it was his voice. Already, she thought she would know those tones anywhere—plain and classless most of the time, save for that occasional Northern hint. But the man by her side was the one she had spotted reading the paper . . . and he didn't tally with the scruffy, bushy-bearded individual she had met earlier.

For a start, this man was clean-shaven, and his hair, although thick and plentiful, had been brushed, and shone with cleanliness. He was the owner of a lean, narrow, intelligent face with quite a purposeful jaw, and beneath a high forehead the blue eyes regarded her with a keen, no-nonsense appraisal. Although no more than average height, he had a long-legged ranginess which made him appear taller, and he wore clean, if well-worn, cord trousers, a white shirt, and a grey sweater from a well-known chain-store back home.

And suddenly, she cursed her own stupidity. 'I'll go and render myself more savoury,' he had said, and yet somehow, ridiculously, she had expected him to return looking much the same.

She forced herself to stop staring at him like an idiot.

'I'm sorry, Dr Wade. I didn't recognise you, for a moment,' she said.

He looked blankly at her, and then let out a hoarse guffaw of indignant humour.

'Good grief, woman, you don't think I regularly walk about looking like the first-prize winner at the tramps' ball?' he demanded unceremoniously. 'I admit I'm not famous hereabouts for my sartorial elegance, but normally I bath and shave! However, I was pushed to keep our appointment here. I'd been up country attending to a birth which turned out to be more complicated than was expected.'

'Up country?' Claire repeated faintly. 'You mean...further up than where you live?'

'Oh, yes. There are some extremely isolated small settlements, high in the mountains. You should see at least one of them if you're to get the picture.'

He took her elbow.

'Come along. We're providing too much excitement for our friend behind the desk. So many *gringos* in one day! And I'd like a drink, I don't know about you.'

'So would I,' Claire said, more feelingly than she had intended, and followed him into the bar.

An apparently ancient woman poured Ashley Wade a shot of the colourless local spirit. Claire asked for whisky-soda and saw the dark eyebrows shoot up.

'That's a relief—I was afraid you'd ask for one of those peculiar mixed-up drinks the girls have back home, which I doubt they've heard of here,' he said. 'Whisky's expensive, though, in Rio Negro. If you're going to drink with me, you had better cultivate a taste for *aguardiente*. So long as you don't let it affect you as it has your photographer.'

'I rarely have enough for it to have that effect,' Claire said, annoyed. She had never before been entertained by a man who dared to tell her what she should drink. 'Are you going to eat here...or have you somewhere less ritzy in mind?' she added, a sharp little dig she could not resist.

He was unperturbed. In fact, he seemed to derive some amusement from her remark.

'Oh, here. Let's push the boat out,' he suggested.

The dining-room of the hotel looked out on the square, where family parties and groups of young people were strolling about with apparent aimlessness. Claire watched them with exaggerated interest. It was a way of avoiding the alert blue eyes of Ashley Wade across the table, and of diverting her own confused reactions to him.

'The nightlife is pretty limited hereabouts,' he observed. 'Apart from the less salubrious establishments which all towns have, this is it. The girls watch the boys, and the boys watch the girls.'

'The *paseo*,' Claire said. 'You still see it, sometimes, in Mediterranean countries.'

'You saw a version of it in the small town in Yorkshire where I grew up,' he said with a grin. 'What will you eat? I recommend that you leave the local specialities alone, and have something fairly plain, like chops and fried potatoes. We don't want you under the weather tomorrow, as well.'

Claire's creamy-white skin reddened.

'Do you always have to be quite so blunt?' she demanded.

He shrugged. 'Where I come from, we call a spade a spade,' he said. 'Shall we risk a carafe of the house red? It's local, but quite drinkable.'

'Why not, since we're pushing the boat out?' Claire said drily. 'They're probably out of Château Latour, anyhow.' Dining out with Dr Ashley Wade was a novel experience, to say the least.

As they were eating, Claire saw two young men come into the dining-room and sit at a table across the room, in clear view of herself and her companion. Something about them jogged her memory, and she recalled that she had seen the pair of them earlier, on the bus. She had noticed them particularly because, although obviously natives of the country, they did not look like peasants, as did most of the passengers. They appeared sharper, more affluent, better, if casually dressed—good American jeans, and modern T-shirts. She had felt, uncomfortably, that they were watching her. Whenever she turned her head, their eyes were looking in her direction, and she felt it again now. It did not help her to relax.

'What's the matter?' Dr Wade asked abruptly, noting her unease.

'Nothing, really...it's just those two men, over there. I noticed them on the bus today.'

He glanced quickly at them.

'Not local. Obviously from the capital,' he said. 'Wonder what they're doing here . . . they don't look like tourists.'

'I'm not terribly interested what their business is,' Claire said tartly. 'I just wish they'd quit watching me. They were doing it on the bus, and now they're at it again. I don't like it.'

'Come on, now, I'm sure you're too much of a woman of the world to be surprised at arousing male interest,' he said sardonically. 'You're a white-skinned blonde— a *rubia*. There aren't too many around here like you. But if it really bothers you so much, I could go and say a few well-chosen words to them.'

'I don't need you to do any such thing!' Claire exclaimed, indignant that he should think she wanted his protection.

'I'm glad to hear it,' said Ashley Wade. 'They might not take too kindly to it, and there are two of them, and only one of me. Would you like coffee?'

'Not here,' she said quickly, instinctively. 'Let's get out—please.'

He appeared surprised by the intensity of her demand, but merely shrugged and acquiesced. 'Very well, if too much admiration makes you uptight, we'll go somewhere else.'

Claire opened her mouth to insist that normal male approbation troubled her not in the least, and she could deal with it either by accepting or ignoring it, but she had sensed something inexplicably different in the intent stares of the two men. But how to make him understand what she found hard to define herself? He would probably only scoff at her and accuse her of schoolgirl nervousness. So she bit her lip and decided to dismiss the entire episode from her mind.

He signalled for the bill, and when it came, on a small ceramic saucer, she hesitated before picking it up. Of course, the meal qualified as a legitimate business expense for which she could claim reimbursement, but she still suffered from a residual apprehension about paying when her companion was male. And, to her mortification, Ashley Wade was fully aware of her uneasiness and the reasons for it.

'Go ahead,' he said cheerfully, pushing the saucer towards her. 'You're the one with the expense account. Don't worry about my ego. I gave up on it long ago.'

Claire struggled with a mixture of emotions as she paid the bill. She had never met anyone remotely like this man. He irritated her immensely, and yet had the ability to make her feel small and insignificant. He was blunt to the point of rudeness, yet she could not convince herself he was totally insensitive. And it irked her that she had sat opposite him for the time it took to eat a meal and found out virtually nothing about him. I'm not doing my job, she thought angrily. In some way he's preventing me from functioning normally, and no man has ever done that before.

'Where are you taking me for coffee?' she challenged as they left the hotel, urged on by a desire to bring him down a peg or two in return. 'The place where you're staying, perhaps?'

'If you insist.' He grinned, seemingly unembarrassable. 'I warn you, it isn't the Waldorf Astoria.'

'At least you must have had running water, which is more than we did at the Principal,' she retorted.

He laughed, that scornfully humorous laughter which so unsettled her.

'Aye,' he said. 'That I did.'

He led her across the square and, once past the church, the streets immediately became darker and narrower.

There had been a blaze of cafés around the square, but here there were only blank walls and shuttered windows, and a silence which was alarming. They were approaching the outskirts of the small town, that much was obvious. The street was now unpaved and uneven, difficult for Claire in her high-heeled sandals. The houses were fewer, with shadowy gaps between them, and the moon, appearing desultorily from behind the clouds, illumined briefly the dark shape of the encircling mountains.

'Where are we going?' she demanded suspiciously. 'There are no hotels here—any fool can see that. I think I'd sooner go back to the town centre.'

'Shut up,' he said. 'Since you were so curious to see where I'm staying, you shall do so. If you go back now, you go alone.'

Claire fumed at the choice with which he had confronted her. She could leave him, but then she would have to walk alone through the silent, darkened, menacing streets, all the way back to the square and the Hotel Principal. She might get lost on the way... or attacked... she had been warned about some of the less pleasant things that could happen to unwary travellers in this part of the world. Or she could reluctantly go along with Ashley Wade, and do as she was told. Angrily, she chose the latter course as the lesser evil... if only just.

But her doubts returned as he led her into a field behind a low adobe building. Somewhere nearby a goat bleated, making her start. And then a shape loomed up, and something warm and hairy brushed against her.

Claire jumped back with a small scream, and would have stumbled over backwards had not Dr Wade's firm hands descended on her shoulders and prevented her from falling.

'You're a real townie, aren't you?' he said amusedly. 'Take it easy—it's only Modesta.'

Out of his pocket he took a torch, and as its beam shone ahead, Claire saw a mule, peacefully cropping the grass. The realisation that she had made such a fuss over bumping into this harmless animal did not make her feel less foolish, or more kindly disposed towards her companion, who she was sure was enjoying her discomfiture.

The moon came out fully, putting the torch out of business, and Claire saw her surroundings clearly, the adobe building which must be someone's dwelling, the mule and a couple of goats contentedly munching, and a tiny, one-man tent in a corner of the field. Realisation came to her, and she looked up at Ashley Wade. He wasn't exactly laughing, but a smile tugged wickedly at the edges of his mouth.

'You're camping?' she said.

He delved into the tent and pulled out a small portable stove, poured water from a plastic container into a battered saucepan, and proceeded to brew up. 'Only one mug, sorry about that, so we'll have to share. Ladies first.'

Claire sipped the hot, strong coffee, black and sugarless.

'Why?' she asked simply.

'Why?' he repeated tauntingly. 'Isn't it fairly obvious, Miss Mallory? I'm practising economy. Camping is cheaper. I have an arrangement with Annunciata, whose house you see back there. As for the bathroom facilities you envied, the hot springs for which the town is named are a short walk away, in the hills. No shortage of hot running water there. I'd have suggested you join me, but I don't know you well enough to offer to scrub your back.'

Something in his tone caused Claire to shiver uncomfortably, and she made a deliberate point of ignoring his last remark.

'Dr Wade, surely you can't be *that* short of money?' she objected. 'If the Principal is the top of the tree, other accommodation in town must be ridiculously cheap.'

'Let's just say I have a mean Yorkshire streak,' he said expressionlessly. 'If there's owt for nowt, I can't resist it. Besides, I have to graze Modesta somewhere, and even the Principal might object to that. Annunciata lets her share the field with the goats.'

'The mule is yours?' Claire was descending ever deeper into puzzlement.

'Naturally. How else do you think I got into town?' he queried, clearly relishing her surprise. 'Well, you could walk, but it's a fair step. I call her Modesta as a sort of Spanish version of Modestine—you know, from R.L. Stevenson's *Travels with a Donkey in the Cevennes*.'

Claire had read the author's account of rough travel in the mountains of Southern France, and her heart began to sink with her understanding of the situation.

'You mean that's the way we are going to travel back, tomorrow?' she said. 'Your letter said you would arrange transportation.'

'So I shall. There's a market in the morning. We should be able to pick up a few *burros* reasonably enough. There's no road worth speaking of,' he explained. 'When you see the terrain, you'll understand. Only a Land Rover might manage to get through. Unfortunately...' He shrugged.

'I know. You can't afford one,' she supplied tartly.

He looked at her long and hard.

'Precisely. That's why you're here, Miss Mallory. Have you finished with the mug?'

She handed it to him.

'Here. And for goodness' sake, call me Claire, won't you? I doubt if all this formality will survive a mule trek into the wilderness.'

As he was finishing his coffee, the door of the house opened, and a short woman with her black hair in two heavy braids stood in a pool of light. Ashley turned to Claire.

'Come and meet my hostess. She would willingly put me up in her house, but as there are seven of them in there, even with her husband away working, I don't feel I should add to the overcrowding.'

Annunciata seemed anxious, but forced a smile as Ashley explained that the *gringa* lady was a reporter from England, who would help him to do more for the poor people. Claire saw at once what he meant about over-crowding. The house was only two rooms, one a small kitchen with an open fire cooking range, the other a living-cum-bedroom. Several children of assorted ages were asleep on truckle beds, leaving little space for the rustic table and chairs. The hard earth floor was covered by a few rush mats, and a kerosene lamp standing on the table provided the only light.

One of the children, a boy of about six or seven, was restless and feverish. He looked exhausted and badly in need of sleep, but tossed and turned, his thin body shaking as a fit of coughing racked it. It was violent and uncontrollable, his face almost blue beneath its natural olive colour, his eyes wide with fear which Claire saw reflected in the worried gaze of his mother.

Ashley Wade knelt by the bed, sat the child up, and held him until the fit subsided, speaking quietly to him in Spanish.

'Poor kid,' Claire said. 'Isn't that whooping cough?'

'Right,' he agreed. 'I've put him on a course of anti-biotics, but what he needs now is a good night's sleep, and he won't get that while he's so terrified by the coughing. I'm going to give him a mild sedative to calm him down, and something to keep the airways open.'

He explained all this carefully to Annunciata, and the two women smiled warily at each other as he treated the boy. Claire could well imagine that her foreign appearance and her air of affluence made her seem like a creature from another planet to this careworn peasant woman. But I'm a woman, just like you, she wanted to say, and her lack of comprehension, her inability to do anything practical to help, made her feel frustrated and angry with herself, in a way that was strange to her.

The child, whose name was Tonio, was much calmer and appeared to be drifting off to sleep when Claire and Ashley left. He walked her back to her hotel through the quiet streets.

'A good job you had your doctor's bag with you—or are you never without it?' she asked.

'Like a carpenter, I'm not much use without my tools,' he said. 'It's not much use my telling you your shelf has fallen down if I can't put it back up. Besides, I told you, I have an arrangement with Annunciata. She lets me use her field, and I treat her family.'

'There's no doctor in Aguas Calientes?'

'There is. But naturally, he charges. There's no state-subsidised medicine in Rio Negro,' he said shortly. 'You can get treated if you can afford it, or are prepared to put yourself into debt.'

Claire thought of the cost of the drugs Ashley Wade had administered to Tonio, in return for...what? A corner of a field and some grazing for the mule. Clearly this barter was unequal, purely a fiction, and she thought that if he practised much of this sort of medicine, it was no wonder he was in dire financial straits.

'Is that how you run your medical service?' she asked. 'I can appreciate that it's difficult for poor families such as Annunciata's to pay for medical care, but——'

He cut her off short. 'You think that's poverty?' he demanded roughly. 'I suppose to you it is. But Annunciata is better off than many. She has a bit of land, some livestock, and her husband is currently in work. They eat—every day—and for some of her children there might even be a future. With a bit of luck, they might possibly be able to put the two eldest through school. Boys, of course. There would be no point for the girls, who will marry young and start having babies immediately.'

His voice was brutally matter of fact, and Claire reacted angrily.

'I hate that sort of thinking! It's so short-sighted. If you educate a woman, her whole family benefits. It's never wasted.'

'That's all very fine and idealistic, but I'm talking sheer, hard economics, Claire,' he said. 'There's not enough return for investment on the girls. The boys will bring money into the household for a few years before they marry, and then they will support families of their own. Out here, you'll have to dispense with your feminist fancies. They simply won't hold up.'

They reached the door of the Hotel Principal just in time for Claire to prevent herself from exploding at having her perfectly reasonable beliefs dismissed as 'feminist fancies'. And in spite of her protests that it wasn't necessary, he insisted on seeing her inside. 'Just to make sure your two...ah...admirers aren't around.'

But the lobby was deserted. The sleepy clerk had finally gone off duty, and the old woman who had earlier been serving in the bar was now knitting behind the desk.

She gave Claire her keys, and, turning to wish him good-night, Claire caught Ashley yawning behind his hand.

At first she was indignant. Was he bored, or just plain rude? Then she remembered he had been 'up country' and had presumably spent several days in the saddle, riding Modesta to Aguas Calientes. It was small wonder he was exhausted, and she promised herself she would try to be more tolerant of his shortcomings, remembering the good, caring side of his nature he had demonstrated at Annunciata's house.

'Goodnight, Dr Wade...Ashley,' she said, offering him her hand. 'I'll see you tomorrow. I hope my colleagues will have recovered by then. They're looking forward to meeting you.'

His grip was so hard, she feared it might crush her fingers.

'Don't lie in too long,' he ordered. 'We have some marketing to do, and I don't intend to be late leaving Aguas Calientes.'

'As a working woman, I'm not in the habit of sleeping late,' she informed him briskly. 'Thank you for an interesting evening.'

'I should be thanking *you*—you bought dinner,' he pointed out. 'Isn't the world topsy-turvy these days? If it had been the other way round, I'd have been expecting a goodnight kiss. Or possibly more.'

She looked sharply at him, expecting to see the wicked grin, but he was resolutely straight-faced.

'I'm not looking for any such recompense,' she assured him. 'Dinner was on the magazine, not me, and is without strings.'

'Perhaps it's as well. My social and other graces are severely out of practice,' he said, and strolled out of the hotel with no more than a parting wave.

Claire knew she should get to sleep at once, in preparation for an arduous day tomorrow. She was certainly worn out, but an evening of Ashley Wade's unsettling company ensured that sleep did not come to order, and two hours later she was still gazing at the ceiling.

A creeping disatisfaction which had afflicted her intermittently for many months came back to nag at her now, as these things so often do during the sleepless small hours. She had suppressed it before, and tried to do so now, telling herself it was without foundation. She had an interesting career that showed every sign of flourishing, a pleasant flat of her own, plenty of friends. Her mirror told her she was attractive to look at, and men frequently confirmed this judgement.

Analysed separately, all these different facets of her life could be said to be satisfactory. Why, then, did the sum total not add up? It was like a Chinese puzzle, with one piece missing. All very nice, she thought, but where's the spark? Was there something she should be doing, and was not? Something she should be feeling, experiencing, getting steamed up about?

She could not kill off the suspicion that these renewed doubts were somehow the result of meeting and talking to the eccentric, enigmatic Dr Ashley Wade. *He* had disturbed her, thrown her off kilter, *he* was at the root of her insomnia tonight. Damn him, Claire thought aggrievedly, as, refusing to trust the hotel reception's promised early call, she set her travelling alarm for six o'clock, and resolutely closed her eyes.

CHAPTER THREE

IF SHE had not suffered such a disturbed night, Claire would not have needed the urgent shrilling of the alarm to wake her next morning. The square outside was full of noise: shouts, cries, laughter, animal sounds—a cacophony of life and activity. Struggling out of bed, she crossed to the window and peered out between two slats of the blinds.

The market was in full swing, stalls so close together the shoppers were almost on top of one another, tended by peasant women in colourful skirts and shawls, and broad-brimmed black hats tied beneath their ample chins. There was pottery and bales of cloth, there were mounds of fruit and vegetables, meat—already swarming with flies, she noted distastefully—and live chickens and goats, protesting vocally against their treatment. She wondered at what unearthly hour the stallholders had set off this morning, particularly those who had trudged in from the surrounding countryside.

Mercifully, there was water in the shower today. Claire spent a grateful interlude under it, since she could not forgo this opportunity to wash her hair. She towelled it and pinned it up—for all its thickness it would dry quickly enough in the heat—then scrambled into jeans and a checked cotton skirt.

A knock on her door revealed Greg, a little pale, but on his feet, and beautifully turned out in perfectly cut denims by a well-known New York designer, an expensive-looking pale blue sweatshirt, and suede casual shoes. He looked just right for a tourist, about to spend

37

an easy day in the country, but rather overdressed for a rough trek.

'Better?' she smiled.

'I'll live,' he conceded grudgingly. 'Have you seen the goings-on outside? When I heard the pandemonium, I was afraid they might be having another of their revolutions.'

'It's called local colour,' said Claire. 'I'm told we must do some buying ourselves this morning. Greg, I wouldn't risk those super trousers, if I were you. They'll be ruined. Haven't you an old pair you could travel in?'

'But these *are* my old ones,' he protested. 'Appearances have to be kept up, Claire, even in odd corners of the globe such as this. I don't enjoy looking disreputable.'

That was a masterly understatement. It was not in his nature to appear less than immaculate.

'OK. But don't say I didn't warn you. We have to ride mule-back for the rest of the journey, apparently.'

He looked suitably shocked. 'You can't be serious?'

'Absolutely. The good doctor told me so himself— among other things. Have you seen Basil yet this morning?'

'Yes. He's feeling rather grim, but at least he's mobile. He says he can't face breakfast, but will join us for coffee. Meanwhile, I'm eager to meet Dr Wade. What room number is he?'

Claire sputtered with laughter. 'Greg, he isn't staying here,' she explained. 'He's camping in a field. I saw it for myself last night.'

He listened, fascinated, as she told him about her visit to Annunciata's house. 'Well, he did say he was short of funds. That's why he wrote to us.'

'Funds, yes—but I assumed he meant for medicine and equipment. But, Greg, he doesn't seem to have two pence to his name,' Claire said slowly. 'If he were a business, he'd be in liquidation.'.

He was thoughtful as they went down to breakfast, and Claire did not interrupt his thoughts. Behind that languid charm and studied elegance lay a sharp, effective business brain, she was sure, or he would not have reached a position of such eminence in his organisation so relatively young. Her job was to write about what they found—his was to work out the financial angle.

She received the first sharp shock of the day on entering the dining-room. Ashley Wade was already seated at one of the tables—not eating or drinking anything, just sitting there—and his face was dark with disapproval. He looked pointedly at his watch as they approached.

'What time do you call this?' he demanded peremptorily, without any introductory preamble, glaring at Claire and ignoring her companion. 'I thought I said early!'

'It's only just after seven,' she objected, angry and defensive.

'Early, in a country that gets as hot as this does by midday, means preferably before sunrise,' he informed her coldly. 'I've been up for three hours, packed, eaten, and negotiated the purchase of three *burros*. Hurry up, or the owner won't hold them for much longer.'

Claire found it difficult to believe anyone could be so downright rude. They had travelled thousands of miles in answer to his call for help, and all he could do was to chide them for being late risers by his standards. He hadn't even had the courtesy to greet Greg Telford, on whose decision his hopes would ultimately rest.

For herself, she did not dare speak, afraid that she would lose her temper so completely that she would have them thrown out of the hotel for causing a disturbance. Greg looked stunned, as if he had been hit by a hurricane. He was used to being shown considerable deference by people older and more influential than this irate, impatient young doctor, and had yet to adjust to this total lack of respect.

It was Basil who saved the situation. Appearing from nowhere, bearded and wearing denims only slightly less worn than Ashley Wade's, he said, 'Hey, man, great to meet you at last. Sorry I was a bit under the weather last night.' He looked from one tense face to another. 'What's the problem?'

'The problem,' Claire said stiffly, 'is that Dr Wade has found three mules for us to ride, and he wants us to rush out and clinch the deal. We, not unnaturally, would like to eat before setting out on such a long journey.'

Basil burst into laughter, then put a hand to his forehead, as if the noise had caused him pain.

'Give him the bread, man,' he said, nudging Greg. 'While you sort that out, doctor, we'll order some coffee.'

'I'm glad someone has some common sense,' Ashley said, looking pointedly at Claire as he accepted the handful of local currency notes Greg fished out of his wallet. Then he disappeared into the thronged market square.

Claire sighed. 'Sorry—I should have warned you he's impossibly rude.'

'Cool it, Claire.' Basil shook his head. 'The guy was in an awkward situation because he didn't have enough to pay for the beasts, and didn't like to ask for it.'

Claire groaned. After last night, she should have known better than anyone that Ashley Wade had no money. Yet she had allowed his manner to upset her. Instead of thinking it out reasonably, she had simply reacted. Somehow, she had got to stop letting him make her hackles rise so easily.

By the time he returned, she and Greg were tucking into fried eggs and toast, and there was a pot of piping hot coffee on the table.

'Done it!' he said with satisfaction, counting out the change meticulously and handing it back to Greg. 'Three healthy, strong-looking animals. I left a boy looking after them, along with my own mule, so let's not take too long. It's costing us.'

By now, Greg had recovered his composure.

'Dr Wade—I suggest you let *me* worry about the expense of this trip. As you yourself pointed out, General Chemicals is not about to go under.'

Ashley looked at him thoughtfully, and the beginnings of a smile brightened his lean face.

'All right,' he agreed. 'One man, one job, I suppose. I'm the doctor, you're the financial expert. It's just that I can't abide waste. What you're paying that boy to mind the mules would be better spent on medical supplies.'

Greg nodded. 'I appreciate your point. But look at it another way—we're supporting the local economy. The boy's family probably need every *peso*.'

'Sure they do. And he'll probably buy himself a Coke, or some revolting, cheap sweets which will rot his teeth,' Ashley said cynically.

There was nothing ill-natured about this exchange, but it struck Claire forcibly that the doctor was not about to concede any point easily. The fact that Greg Telford could say yea or nay to supporting his enterprise would not, she realised, affect his behaviour in any way. He would continue to be as argumentative or as plain bloody-minded as he chose. He simply did not have it in him to kow-tow, or creep, or, to put it in more civilised language, to 'cultivate' anyone. She wondered how many people's backs he had put up with this attitude, and if Greg's were broad enough to take it.

'How's Tonio today?' she asked, breaking in on the discussion before it became an argument.

'He's a lot better. Tonio will make it. As you probably know, whooping cough is most dangerous under the age of one year. But I can't be there for *all* the Tonios, damn it!' he burst out frustratedly.

'It seems to me that you need the backing of a big organisation, like the WHO,' Greg said slowly.

'I agree. But the government here is decidedly reluctant to ask for outside help. It would be tantamount to admitting that all wasn't perfect, and owning up to deficiencies might encourage another coup. See? It's a vicious circle.'

'I do see. But *I'm* here, and obviously I'm not going to be secretive about what I'm doing. Claire's magazine will see that my company will get maximum publicity.'

'I didn't pick General Chemicals with a pin and my eyes closed,' Ashley said baldly. 'You've got a number of subsidiaries operating in Rio Negro, which makes you a big, influential employer. I figured the authorities wouldn't want to annoy you.' His head jerked suddenly in Claire's direction. 'Got all that, have you? I haven't seen you taking any notes, and you aren't along just for the ride.'

Through gritted teeth, she said, 'You do your job in your way, Dr Wade, and kindly let me do mine as I see fit.' And then she concentrated on pouring more coffee, avoiding the mockery alight in the blue eyes.

The next few hours were spent frantically trying to buy everything they needed. The journey would take them more than two days, and would involve sleeping in the open, but they only managed to acquire one more tent. Claire wondered fleetingly about the sleeping arrangements, but deliberately refrained from bringing up the subject. Then there were sleeping-bags, rucksacks and saddlebags for their clothes and belongings, since you couldn't, as Ashley pointed out, carry a suitcase on muleback, and essential food rations for the journey.

'I take it we won't be able to buy anything en route?' Greg said, with a nervous gleam in his eyes. Claire thought his idea of rural isolation was probably Clapham Common, or New York's Central Park.

'Not a lot. There won't be any supermarkets,' Ashley agreed. He glanced down at Greg's suede casuals. 'You'll need some stronger footwear than those bordello-creepers, old son. Apart from the fact that they'll disintegrate, they wouldn't offer much protection if you stepped on a snake.'

The word 'snake' made them all shudder automatically, and they invested in stout boots without demur, although Greg winced at the unflattering effect on his appearance.

Finally, they collected the mules—patient, stolid animals, smelling slightly rank—and under Ashley's direction everything was carefully packed and loaded.

Claire, tightening the fasteners on her saddlebag, happened to glance up, and an inexplicable shiver ran down her spine. Across the square, drinking outside one of the cafés, but watching nevertheless, were the two men she had seen in the hotel last night, and on the bus earlier yesterday. About to reach out and touch Ashley's arm to draw his attention to them, she thought better of it. Two men are watching me . . . it sounded so silly, so infantile, even though she could not accept the obvious explanation that they were looking at her simply because she was young, blonde and female.

She turned her back on them firmly. She would be free of their unpleasant observation soon enough, and why give Ashley Wade another excuse for being impatient, scathing or...worse...finding humour at her expense?

The sun beat down vengefully from a fierce, bright sky, and the heat was already scarcely bearable, as the little cavalcade mounted up and moved slowly through the crowded streets, mules and shoppers jostling one another.

'Hey, man!' Basil protested as Greg's mule bumped into his. 'Didn't you tell me you were an experienced rider?'

'Horses, Basil. Decent animals with at least a proportion of Arab in them. Not these degenerate creatures!' Greg muttered fastidiously.

Claire kept her gaze fixed on Ashley's back, straight and yet relaxed in the saddle, as the last scattered houses of Aguas Calientes fell away behind them. Ahead was the rough trail, and miles of rugged country, with the mountains shimmering in the heat, fold upon fold, like a convoluted piece of crumpled parchment. It looked wild and forbidding, and she shuddered, finding it difficult to believe that people lived in that scorched, remote vastness. She felt as though she were leaving civilisation irretrievably behind, and would never again return to the routine of normal living.

And yet, for Ashley Wade, this life was normal, was routine. What kind of man exiled himself in this manner, embracing hardship and loneliness and separation from his own people? What motives drove him to do so? It occurred to Claire that the human aspect of the story she had been sent to cover was just as fascinating as the medical, and she saw that this might be the angle from which she should approach it—the need, the hour, producing the man. But she doubted very much that this particular man would make the task easy for her.

The hills in the immediate vicinity of Aguas Calientes were entirely covered by the glossy green-leaved bushes of coffee plantations in neatly regimented rows, being tended by industrious workers. There were beautiful white *haciendas* with red-tiled roofs and lush gardens, and Claire caught the occasional blue glimpse of a swimming pool as they passed.

'The plantation managers live in some style,' Ashley said drily. 'Why not? They can pay rock-bottom wages for cheap labour without redress, knowing that they can hire and fire with impunity. The trouble is that most of the productive land in this country belongs to government interests, big foreign companies, and a few wealthy families, none of whom provide much in the way of medical care for their workers, incidentally. There's an average life expectancy of fifty, widespread infant mortality, and more or less general malnutrition.'

'Why do they stand for it?' Basil muttered. 'Seems like what these guys need is a change of government.'

Ashley gave a snort of scornful amusement. 'They get that all too regularly! It's a case of *"Plus ça change, plus c'est la même chose."* Everything changes, and yet remains the same. A different general, a new dictator, but the real power stays in the same hands, and nothing improves the lot of the vast majority of the populace.'

Very soon they left the coffee *fincas* behind, and rode into a different world. There was the occasional poor farm, where a family tried to eke out subsistence from the stubborn soil, and then nothing but scrub, hills and sky. As they climbed higher, Claire glanced back over her shoulder and could see for mile after mile of emptiness. The same prospect seemed to lie ahead.

They stopped to rest out the hottest part of the day beneath the meagre shade of a clump of trees, and to eat the bread, cheese and fruit they had brought at the

market that morning. Ashley was silent and uncom-
municative. He leaned back against Modesta's re-
cumbent form, tipped forward the brim of his hat, and
gave every appearance of having gone to sleep.

Claire found this intensely annoying. They were here
at his request, and the least he could do was talk to them,
and not behave as if they weren't there at all.

'I must say, you make a really entertaining host,' she
muttered aggrievedly, eyeing his inert form. 'How about
a little scintillating conversation?'

'It's wiser to conserve your energy,' he remarked
dampeningly from beneath his hat. 'Talking only dis-
sipates it. Get some rest. We have a long way to go today,
thanks to our late departure.'

The rebuke was well-grounded but none the less ir-
ritating and, lost for a suitable retort, she was obliged
to subside. They all relapsed into a stupefied, semi-
comatose torpor, the long, hot silence disturbed only by
the buzzing of bees and the chirping of insects in the
grass. Later in the afternoon, when the sun's ferocity
had eased a little, they mounted up and rode on.

Claire's denimed legs rubbed against the rough hide
of her mule's flank, and in spite of her precautionary
lathering of high-factor sun oil, and the careful covering
of most of her body with protective clothing, there was
a patch on the back of her wrist where her hand rested
as she held the reins which had caught the sun and was
burning angrily. She felt stiff and saddle-sore as, at last,
the red ball sinking in a sky of liquefied magenta behind
the darkening ridge of hills, Ashley Wade decided they
would stop for the night.

The place he chose was obviously one he knew well
and had used before, a small valley in the protective
shade of a steep cliff, with acacia trees and a patch of
grass greener than the thorny yellow scrub they had

traversed all afternoon. The reason for this was the small stream, little more than a trickle, which oozed soporifically through it. There was even a pile of stones, roughly constructed to form a makeshift fireplace, which showed signs of previous use.

'Anyone been in the Scouts—or Guides, as the case may be?' he queried cheerfully. 'I'm not using my camping stove fuel unnecessarily. Collect up as much dry wood as you can find.'

'I'll gladly reimburse you for the fuel, if that's a problem,' Greg declared.

Ashley shook his head. 'Thanks, but no. It's best to live off the land while we can. The fuel, like many other things, has to be carted up from Aguas. There's no delivery service.'

Thus Claire was treated to a sight she never would have expected—the elegant executive in his designer denims, scrambling about on the slopes, hunting for twigs and bits of wood. She couldn't resist a smile as she joined in the search.

Remarkably quickly, Ashley had a fire going, and everyone found themselves peeling and chopping potatoes, onions and peppers. With the addition of some dried meat, which looked as appetising as rubber until it was combined with liquid in the pan, a surprisingly tasty stew was produced. Even allowing for the fact that a day of physical exercise in the open air had made them hungry enough to eat just about anything, the meal, rounded off with fresh oranges and coffee, was more enjoyable than Claire would have dreamed.

'Have you always been such an accomplished cook?' she asked, with only a hint of sarcasm.

'Always,' he said cheerfully. 'There's no better training than being a junior doctor on a pitiful salary, in a one-room bedsit. What I didn't know, I learned fast.' He looked down at her arm. 'Got a bit burned, haven't you? They shouldn't send people with your colouring to Rio Negro.'

'I'm not employed for my skin colour,' she retorted, stung by his attitude. 'Unfortunately they didn't happen to have a suitably qualified West Indian or Nigerian journalist, so you'll have to put up with me.'

'OK, keep your hair on.' He grinned, reaching for his pack. 'I've got some calamine lotion in here. It's still better for sunburn than all those new-fangled preparations. If you go round the other side of the cliff you'll find that the stream forms a small pool where it's possible to wash.'

Claire followed his directions. The pool was shallow, but at least private. In fact, although the others were not more than twenty yards away, she was aware of a deep sense of isolation, of being alone with the mountains, the night sky and the trees. The only sounds were the cries of night hunting birds, and the rustlings of small, unidentified creatures in the grass. Thankfully, she stripped off her jeans, shirt and bra, and splashed herself with the water which was deliciously cool.

She heard him approach. The off-key whistling of an old pop song was not the call of any bird, although from the way the blood rushed alarmingly through her veins she might have been the victim of a predator. Standing there in just her lacy briefs, with her arms crossed over her breasts, she felt both foolish and vulnerable.

'You could have given me a few minutes longer before demanding the bathroom facilities!' she gasped furiously. 'Or are you a closet peeping Tom?'

'Peeping Toms hide behind rocks. I gave clear warning of my approach,' he said. He didn't avert his gaze, but regarded her openly, and she felt herself grow hot and confused. 'Don't worry—there's more to be seen on any public beach these days. It just occurred to me that you might have painful spots you didn't care to mention, so I brought you some ointment for...er...saddle-soreness.'

He held out the tube, a little teasingly, she thought, since he was well aware both her hands were occupied. She glared at him, motionless, and he shrugged, grinned wryly, and dropped it on the ground by her clothes before turning and walking away, still whistling the same tune.

Struggling with a strange mixture of anger and excitement she found hard to understand, Claire dried herself and pulled on her clothes. He was a doctor, wasn't he? And certainly he did not seem overcome by the sight of her half-naked. Did she want him to be? Certainly not, she insisted firmly, pulling herself together before going back to join the others.

She found them putting up the two tents.

'You and Basil can share one, Greg, and Claire can have the other,' Ashley directed. 'I'll sleep in the open. I often do, anyhow, and I'm used to it.' Catching sight of Claire, he said, 'I expect you're relieved to learn you aren't expected to share with me.'

'Not in the least—since I'd no intention of doing so,' she replied coldly. Did he really think she would not exercise any choice in the matter?

Greg went off to wash, carrying his sponge-bag and towel for all the world as though he were in a four-star hotel, and, while Ashley brewed some more coffee over the fire, Basil rooted anxiously through his pack and saddlebags.

'Man, there was a half-bottle of Scotch in here, this morning! Now I can't lay my hands on it!'

'Oh, that,' Ashley said, with a casual shrug. 'I left it in Aguas Calientes.'

Basil looked ready to explode. 'You did *what*?'

Ashley poured coffee into tin mugs. He sat comfortably cross-legged on the ground, apparently unperturbed by the other man's agitation.

'It seemed to me your pack was far too heavy. All those rolls of film and equipment. You needed more space, and the whisky seemed the most expendable item. I gave it to the man who sold us the mules, as a tip. After all, he gave us a good deal.'

Basil was virtually incoherent with frustration, and it was some time before he could speak.

'Man, any place I'm going, I need some Scotch! You had no business doing that,' he choked out finally. 'You've pulled my life support system out from under me!'

Ashley shrugged again, treating Basil's protestations as if they were meant in jest.

'Sorry about that. I didn't realise it was so vital. Simmer down, lad, and have some coffee.'

Claire held her breath. Basil, in his normal state, was the most peaceable of souls. When he had been drinking, he was expansive, sociable...and then sleepy. Deprived, he was unpredictable, and she wondered what would be the result of a confrontation out here in the middle of nowhere. Having precipitated the situation, could Ashley cope? He certainly looked calm and unworried, and had not even set down his coffee-mug.

There was a long, uncertain moment. Then Basil gave a gesture of disgust, turned his back and crawled sulkily into his tent.

Claire looked searchingly at Ashley.

'You did that deliberately, didn't you?' she accused, torn between concern and anger. 'Not that I approve of excessive drinking, but Basil is a first-rate photographer, and so long as he does his job, who are we to interfere with his life? He's an adult, after all.'

He shot her an interrogative glance which made her catch her breath at its latent contempt.

'So it's all right if he has a blistering headache tomorrow, trips his mule over the edge of a cliff, and injures himself? It's all right if he slows our progress and makes the journey more difficult for the rest of us?' he said forcefully. 'Out here, you need your wits about you in order to survive. I've had to watch him as if he were a baby today. And I seriously question the ethics of letting anyone harm himself because it's his own business. It isn't. Each one of us is his brother's keeper.'

He was staring at her with a cold, hard scorn in those keen eyes, as if she were some idiot girl who knew nothing, and it was his mission to put sense into her head. Claire resented his assumption that he had a monopoly of right-thinking, and she yearned to deflate his arrogance with a well-earned pinprick. What had he said last night about having no ego? Oh, but he had ... a colossal, overweening confidence in his own rectitude!

'Is that why you came out here, Dr Wade?' she demanded softly, but scathingly. 'Was it easier here for you to play God?'

His face darkened, and for a moment she thought he was going to seize her, and shake her. She knew a tremor of fear which was also triumph, because at last she had forced a reaction from him. But it was short-lived; he shook his head, dismissing her taunt as unimportant.

'Get back on your island,' he said coolly. 'Before you start on *my* reasons for what I do, best examine your own.'

Without knowing anything about her, how had he managed to put his finger so unerringly on a troublesome pulse? As she watched him dashing out the grounds of his coffee, his back turned as if he had already forgotten her existence, Claire was the one left feeling deflated.

They had been riding for several hours before an isolated cottage, little more than a shack, with adobe walls and a thatched roof came into view, like a mirage in the middle of nowhere. But there were chickens scratching about in the soil, and the diminutive figures of two small children appeared in the doorway as they approached.

All they were able to buy here were eggs and bread and a little fresh fruit, and, as Claire had expected, no money changed hands. By the time they moved off again, Ashley's barter system had provided an appropriate treatment for threadworms in one of the children, and the syringing of his mother's ears to remove wax inside. The poor woman had been convinced she was going deaf, and was absurdly grateful for this simple remedy.

'She looks chronically exhausted,' Claire observed, glancing back at the woman standing in the doorway watching them depart, as if this were the only contact she had had with the outside world in weeks. 'Surely she had that youngest child rather late in life?'

'Not really. She might look nearer fifty, as you would if you'd lived her life, but she's only thirty-four,' Ashley said. 'It's unwise to pass snap judgements. How old are you—mid-twenties? I could easily say you're leaving it rather late to produce your first.'

'If you're assuming that's a failure on my part, then you *are* making a snap judgement,' she retorted. 'Perhaps I simply don't want to.'

His gaze rested on the blonde twist of hair tied back from her face, brushing her shoulders beneath the black hat, and she knew he was thinking of last night, by the stream, when he said caustically, 'No, indeed. It might spoil your figure.'

'It might threaten my independence,' she shot back at him. Why should she take the trouble to explain that she had never met a man she cared sufficiently about to want to become the mother of his children? It was no business of his, and she owed him no explanations. Nor had he any right to make her feel guilty because the fortunate circumstances of her birth had not obliged her to lose her youth and her looks before she was twenty. None of this poverty and hardship was her fault!

They had risen very early that morning, but she had been glad to crawl, stiff and cold, out from the tent in which she was convinced only extreme tiredness had made it possible for her to sleep at all. After a quick brew of coffee they had packed up and got under way before the sun was properly risen. There had been little in the way of conversation. Ashley was brisk and efficient, Greg subdued and thoughtful, and Basil in a sour mood owing to his enforced teetotalism the night before. Claire was more than willing to refrain from talking. At this point in time, she was almost ready to concede that this entire undertaking was misconceived.

After a lunch-time fry-up of eggs and tomatoes, they all began to feel marginally more human. Basil, becoming alive to the drama of the landscape, took some pictures, and Greg began to question Ashley about their destination.

'This place where you live...the village...how large is it?'

'I wouldn't dignify it by that name. San Stefano is no more than a hamlet—a scattered collection of houses surrounded by the fields the people work. Up in the hills beyond there are similar small communities, and odd farms and cottage like the one we passed this morning. There's no church, no shops, no inns, unless you count one rather rough *cantina*. There's a small school, but no teacher. The last one died, and as yet they haven't been able to persuade anyone to accept the job. Until I arrived, there was no doctor closer than Aguas Calientes . . . and he doesn't do house calls! These people have simply been forgotten . . . written off.'

'Wouldn't they do better to abandon the struggle and move to the cities?'

'Many have done so. But for what? There isn't work or housing for them all—you must have seen the apalling shanty towns around the capital.'

'Aren't *you* sometimes tempted to abandon the struggle and go back to being a GP in England?' Claire asked. She had kept out of the conversation so far, but curiosity overcame the resentment she had been nursing since the previous night.

'Sometimes I can scarcely restrain myself,' he replied sarcastically. 'I'm burning up with impatience to spend my time dishing out tranquillisers, and explaining to the mums who drive up in their Volvos that it isn't necessary to give their infants penicillin at the first sign of a sniffle!'

Claire flushed, finding herself once again the target of his mockery.

'It isn't all like that! You're exaggerating grossly. My father was a GP, and every patient he treated wasn't a hypochondriac. He served a real need, did a worthwhile job . . . without being contemptuous of the people who sought his help!'

Ashley Wade brushed aside her admonition.

'Since you admired your father so much, and thought so highly of his work . . . to say nothing of being so knowledgeable about medical matters,' he said sardonically, 'I wonder why you didn't follow in your father's footsteps and become a doctor yourself?'

Claire had not expected him to challenge her in this manner, almost as if he had read the inner secrets of her mind, and knew exactly where to probe in order to cause the greatest distress. His words sent her reeling back through the years, and once again she was fifteen, and re-living the horror of the train crash. Ambulances, their lights flashing, their horns blaring—paramedics rushing back and forth with stretchers—people groaning, screaming with agony, crying out for help—blood everywhere, broken bodies, twisted limbs—death. And, amidst the chaos and anguish, her own bright dreams of the future in ruins all around her, she had stood helpless, whispering senselessly, 'It's no use, I can't, I can't!' Knowing that she could never, never cope with the possibility of pain and terror like this, every day of her life. Knowing she must dash her beloved father's hopes, as well as her own. She did not have what it took to be a doctor...the courage, the stamina, the calm in the face of suffering.

Jumping to her feet, she glared resentfully at Ashley Wade, whose eyes so forcefully sought the truth.

'That,' she declared icily, 'is none of your damned business—*Dr* Wade!'

CHAPTER FOUR

To be fair to him, Ashley Wade had not attempted to paint a glamourised picture of San Stefano for his visitors. He had, in fact, bent in the opposite direction.

'If you're envisaging some picturesque, idyllic scene of rustic tranquillity, complete with poor but contented peasantry, forget it,' he told them roughly. 'You wouldn't choose San Stefano for a postcard, or one of those blow-ups on travel agents' walls. Even from a distance, it isn't all that prepossessing. On closer acquaintance you'll find it squalid, impoverished and unappealing. There's no running water or electricity. The sewage stinks. The people aren't content, simply resigned . . . it's a narcosis of despair.'

Claire had reacted perversely to this stark representation. It couldn't be *that* bad, she thought. Most probably he was deliberately painting it blacker than it really was. He would derive a grim amusement for instilling in them all an even greater fear and trepidation about the conditions awaiting them, and at the back of her mind lurked the uncharitable suspicion that this was in his interests—the worse they were led to believe things were, the greater the amount of financial support he could endeavour to enlist.

'We're not expecting Utopia, or Xanadu,' she informed him briskly, and he shot her a savagely humorous grin.

'I'm relieved to hear it,' he said laconically, and allowed the subject to lapse.

The sun was fierce and hot in the afternoon sky as they caught their first sight of San Stefano. They all had to screw up their eyes as they followed the direction of Ashley's pointing finger, seeing nothing to begin with but the sun-baked hills. Gradually they made out that what they had first taken for rock formations were actually dwellings, so much a part of their background that they looked to have grown organically from they same ochre-coloured stone.

They crossed the bed of a river with a mere trickle of water running through it, and Claire saw men and women working in the fields, bent double in the ferocious heat, shoulders hunched, faces wizened. One man drove a ramshackle plough pulled by a pair of emaciated oxen, others used a primitive contraption she had never seen before, which relied entirely on the power of human limbs and sweat.

'It's a foot plough,' Ashley told her. 'A remnant of the ancient civilisations before the horse and the ox came to these parts. You can still see it all over South America, I believe. Damn hard work, but cheaper. You don't have to feed the ox.'

'What are they growing?' Greg asked.

'Mostly maize, potatoes, cassava—that sort of thing. There's too much carbohydrate in their diet, not enough protein, and a crippling scarcity of green vegetables. The irrigation's poor, you see, the soil is thin and the water supply unreliable.'

The people in the fields briefly stopped work to stare blankly at them as they passed. No one smiled or offered a shout of greeting; there was a sullen, indifferent silence which Claire found menacing, and she looked quickly at the English doctor, trying to elicit something from his reaction.

He raised one hand in a laconic salutation, and in response received a few unrevealing nods of acknowledgement.

'Strewth!' exclaimed Basil. 'It's hardly a rapturous welcome, is it? I mean—well, they don't know us, but man, I would have thought that you were a cross between Dr Barnardo and the Archangel Gabriel around here.'

'I can't imagine what gave you that idea,' Ashley said levelly. 'Not me, certainly. So far as they are concerned, I'm just the cranky foreign quack who can't cure half their ills. After two years, I'm only scratching the surface, and I don't think they really trust me to stay. Every time I go into Aguas, I reckon they think I won't come back. And when I do, they conclude that I must be mad.'

The mules plodded slowly up the dirt track that formed the main street of the village. Here, all was shrouded in the heavy silence of mid-afternoon. From open doorways, a few black-shawled old women watched their progress without comment, and scruffy, big-eyed children peered from behind their skirts. On one corner, a man leaning against a wall stared from beneath the brim of his black hat with an apathy that was almost hostile.

'*Buenos tardes*, José,' Ashley said pleasantly, receiving no more than the briefest of nods as an answer. 'I delivered his wife of twins a month ago, and I get the impression he blames me because there are two more mouths to feed, instead of one,' he added in an aside to his companions. 'It's rare in such confinements for both to survive hereabouts. That's eight José and Conchita have, to date.'

'Room for a vigorous programme of birth control, perhaps?' Claire could not resist querying sweetly.

'Easy enough to say. I do try. But if the priest comes up from Aguas, he'll have me for stewmeat, and if he stirs things up with his superiors, the authorities will sling me out, lock, stock and proverbial barrel,' Ashley rejoined promptly.

Claire set her mouth firmly and tried not to wrinkle her nose. She hated to admit it, but it seemed he had told them no more than the plain truth about San Stefano. She had come to recognise the smell of inadequate sanitation exacerbated by heat, and here it was so strong as to be unbearable. Everyone she saw had the thin, strung-out look of permanent undernourishment, from the workers in the fields, through the children with their stick-like arms and legs, to the mangy, yellow-eyed dogs that slunk along the narrow alleys and growled half-heartedly at them as they passed.

Like Basil, she had had visions of a grateful flock cheerfully welcoming the return of its devoted physician, but it wasn't like that at all. The atmosphere was full of a suspicious surliness, the dull lethargy of a numbed acceptance of hardship. It was depressing in the extreme, and Claire wondered again about Ashley Wade. How could he stand it? Without even the reward of thanks, lacking money and resources and any hope of improvement, how could he bear to remain in this benighted spot?

'I'd offer you a penny for them if I weren't a bit strapped for cash,' he said softly in her ear, riding up close alongside her.

Claire started, and looked searchingly at him.

'I was wondering about you,' she said. 'No one pays you, no one thanks you, and you plainly aren't a saint. So why do you stay?'

'Oh, it's not all bad,' he said lightly. 'Give it a few days, and perhaps you'll begin to understand. And when you do, you can explain it to me,' he added with irony.

Suddenly he snatched the reins of her mule and jerked her out of the way as a shower of foul-smelling water cascaded from an upper window.

'Gardy loo!' he said with a grin.

'Oh, my lord!' Greg muttered with deep distaste, side-stepping his mount so quickly that it narrowly missed a squawking chicken that ran across his path.

'This place is a cesspit,' he murmured, half under his breath. 'What it really needs is the bulldozers in. You'll never have good health here, Ashley, until you demolish all these hovels and build some with twentieth-century plumbing.'

'I'm inclined to agree with you, old son,' the doctor affirmed equably. 'But since it's not likely to happen, we're stuck with what we have.'

'Oh, boy!' Basil said gloomily. 'Is there anywhere a man can get a drink?'

Between short bursts of almost manic picture-taking, he had been alternately edgy and depressed for the past two days, and Claire questioned the soundness of Ashley's tactics in depriving him of his usual solace. She watched him now as he considered this desperate appeal with an unconcern which appeared casual.

'There's a *cantina* of sorts up one of the back alleys, but I wouldn't recommend it,' he said. 'Most of the spirit is home brewed and quite lethal—literally so, if taken in large enough quantities.'

'How come you haven't forbidden your patients to touch the stuff?' Basil challenged resentfully.

'I'm not in a position to forbid,' Ashley pointed out. 'I can, and do, discourage. But these people lead lives of such mind-destroying hardship and poverty, I can't blame them too strongly for resorting to anything that temporarily eases their lot—even when, in the long term, the results are quite the reverse.'

'I sure could do with something to ease my lot, right now!' the photographer muttered sarcastically.

Ashley half turned in the saddle, and his eyes shot contemptuous blue sparks which seemed to include all of them in their fire.

'The worst you've got to endure is a week or two's rough living,' he said scathingly. 'After that, you'll be back in the fleshpots of so-called civilisation. So you'll excuse me if my heart doesn't bleed for you.'

He turned his back on them and dug his knees authritatively into his mule's flanks, urging the beast on up the narrow street through the village.

There was no need for him to be quite so hard on them all, Claire thought resentfully. Didn't he realise that the heat, the dirt, the always visible deprivation, had afflicted them all with a severe case of culture shock? On top of all that, she wondered how she was going to cope with the rude, abrasive persona of Ashley Wade.

As though he felt her eyes boring into his back, he slowed down, allowing her to come up alongside him. The village was beginning to peter out now, and here, away from the limited supply of water, there were no more cultivated fields. The ground was scrubby grass, rising gradually towards yet another range of high hills, the track trailing off into the distance.

'If that was San Stefano, would you mind telling me where we are going?' she asked wearily.

'Patience, lass,' he said annoyingly, and headed his mule off the track in the direction of a clump of acacia trees. As they approached, Claire saw what the copse had previously concealed—a low, squat building reminiscent of the farmsteads they had passed along the way.

'That's where you live?' She sounded doubtful.

'Right. The man who lived in it gave up the struggle to make the land pay, and went to work on the coffee estates,' he said. 'The house was pretty dilapidated when I took it over, but it had the virtue of a well, once I'd cleared it, and plenty of space, and I discovered a talent for dry-stone-walling.'

She had a sudden, disturbing vision of Ashley, hot, grimy and determined, repairing the crumbling walls with his bare hands. Was there no limit to this man's resolve, no ends to which he would not go in pursuit of his purpose? Certainly, the building looked robust enough now, with wooden shutters at the windows and a stout wooden door, but it seemed forbidding rather than welcoming. She knew no relief at journey's end, only an increasing apprehension.

'Welcome to the pleasure-dome,' Ashley Wade said, dismounting easily from his mule. 'It's hardly Xanadu, I know.'

Claire recalled her own glib words with some irritation, annoyed by the way he tossed them easily back at her, and unable to place the source of the quotation—as he obviously could. She slid from the back of her mount, aching in every limb and sore in places she did not care to mention, and it was little consolation to her to note that her two fellow sufferers did not look any happier or less fatigued than she felt.

'Be it never so humble,' their host said facetiously, pushing open the door. He strode inside, flinging back the shutters to let in air and light.

The room was fairly large, but none the less the atmosphere was close and stuffy from the heat. The floor was thick with several days' dust, and particles of it hung suspended in the sunlight streaming in.

'Pilar hasn't been for at least a week, I reckon,' Ashley said philosophically. 'She's supposed to keep the place clean, but I'm pretty sure she never comes near when I'm away.'

Claire's gaze moved restlessly around the dwelling, and she decided that there was very little required in the way of housework for the simple reason that the place contained only the minimum of furnishings and possessions. A couple of roughly woven rugs and rush mats on the floor, chairs and a table of the rough-hewn kind she had seen in Annunciata's house in Aguas Calientes. A kind of couch with a brightly woven blanket flung over it, one or two wooden chests. On the walls, the only adornments were the doctor's framed certificates and diplomas, and one solitary picture—a reproduction Lowry of matchstick figures outside a factory gate. The only refinement was a home-made bookshelf made of planks of wood supported by square-cut blocks of stone, which filled most of one wall. Ashley was obviously a reader. There couldn't be very much else to do here, outside the work, Claire imagined.

'You've been away for some time, but there's no lock on your door,' she observed.

'What would be the sense?' he asked. 'I've nothing worth stealing, other than books, and no one reads English. That door over there is the only one that locks—it's my surgery and drug-store. I can't risk anyone helping themselves to what's in there. It might be dangerous, and furthermore, I can't afford to replace anything.'

The crooked grin tugged at his mouth again.

'You can see the medical facilities, such as they are, tomorrow. Right now, you can all look lively. Greg—there's a fenced field round the back, so since you're the equine expert, you can see to the mules. Basil—bring some water from the well. You'll find it out there, through the kitchen. Claire——' he slung her a long-handled broom '—give the floor a sweep. This place is filthy.'

For a disbelieving moment they all gaped at him, open-mouthed. They'd been two days in the saddle and two nights sleeping rough, and no sooner had they arrived than he expected them to set to and work. Not even the work they had come fully prepared to do, but menial tasks. Claire was particularly incensed that, as the only female in the party, she had deliberately been allotted the duty that Ashley considered befitted her status, and her blood boiled furiously at this chauvinistic treatment.

'You might give us chance to catch our breath!' she complained bitterly.

'I might,' he agreed, 'but you're not at the Ritz now. No room service with hot and cold running flunkeys.'

She glared at him, her initial dislike reactivating itself fiercely.

'And what are *you* going to do while we're all jumping around doing your bidding? Sit and watch, like a pasha?'

He regarded her scornfully. 'Not exactly. I'm going to light the stove. It's temperamental, and positively antediluvian, so if you want to swap jobs, I'm agreeable. But I might point out that we won't get so much as a cup of coffee unless I can coax it to work.'

Greg shrugged wearily. 'Let's get busy, Claire. The sooner we sort ourselves out, the sooner we can get ourselves cleaned up,' he said hopefully.

Claire wielded the broom with a fervour born of angry frustration, furious not only with Ashley for treating them as if they were hired labour, not well-paid professionals whose help he had actively sought, but with herself for reacting so predictably to his brusque manner. Why couldn't she just disregard it and treat all this as a temporary discomfort which would soon be at an end?

It wasn't that she objected to sweeping floors—she did her own housework without thinking it below her—it was being ordered about so high-handedly by this eccentric and ill-mannered individual that irked her.

She swept all the dust out of the door, observing sourly that the welcome breeze which had sprung up would very soon blow it all back in again. In the background she could hear Ashley's voice from the lean-to kitchen, coaxing the primitive range to glowing life with the added persuasion of a number of colourful curses to which she paid no outward attention. If he thought that was going to make her blush, he was sadly mistaken. Anyone who spent her working life brushing shoulders with male journalists was not likely to be embarrassed by a few swear-words.

'Man, that well is straight out of the Bible!' Basil exclaimed, heaving in the wooden bucket. Claire returned the broom to the kitchen, and watched as Ashley tipped water into an iron saucepan.

'Do you cook on that thing as well?' she asked incredulously.

Dirt-smeared, he stood back and surveyed the crackling wood behind the bars, feeding the flames with lumps of charcoal.

'Executive types in the Home Counties do this kind of cooking for fun on their patios at weekends,' he said sardonically. 'They call it barbecuing. This model comes complete with an oven, but I leave that strictly to Pilar—when she turns up.'

The water began to bubble, and Ashley made coffee, pouring it into earthenware mugs.

'This is one luxury I can't seem to give up,' he commented wryly.

Claire stared at him. 'Luxury? The stuff grows here, all over the place. We passed through acres of it outside Aguas Calientes,' she said.

From the way he looked at her, with mingled scorn and pity, she knew instantly she had said something stupid, as she seemed fated to do every time she spoke to him.

'It's available, but at a price,' he said witheringly. 'Surely you realise that these crops are grown for the lucrative export market? They don't benefit the local population, and the money they earn pays for all those fancy *haciendas* you were admiring, with swimming pools, and Range Rovers parked alongside. Personally, I'd dig up all the coffee and plant soya beans.'

'Man, you are a revolutionary,' Basil said uneasily. 'Isn't that kind of talk enough to get you slung into gaol?'

'It might, if my views were considered important,' Ashley smiled. 'Who listens to a crazy foreign doctor? My mother always said I should learn when to "shut my gob", as she phrased it. I'm working on it.'

'But not too hard,' Claire rejoined promptly, without thinking.

The dark blue eyes fixed themselves thoughtfully on her, and irrationally she found herself noticing what thick, dark lashes he had. There was no way you could call that narrow, intelligent face conventionally good-looking, but neither could you deny the compelling quality about it. He'd been here for two years. Was there a woman somewhere, waiting for him? With a rush of embarrassment, she realised she was staring at him, returning his regard as thoroughly as she was receiving it, and she looked away quickly.

All of them were disgustingly filthy, and eager to clean up, but as Ashley warned them, the 'amenities' were not impressive. The shower-room was a covered lean-to out the back, where one stood and tipped the contents of a bucket over one's body.

'One bucket only, mind you,' Ashley said cautioningly. 'The well is only shallow, and sometimes runs dry. Until the rains come, water is at a premium.'

'You can't be expected to live like this,' Greg said seriously, but Ashley only shrugged.

'Millions do.'

'I know, and although that's regrettable, they, at least, are used to it, and haven't known anything different. But you are the product of a more affluent society, and shouldn't be obliged to live like a third-world peasant. Better conditions for the doctor would be one of the first priorities of any collaboration between us.'

'No!' Ashley slammed his fist down on the table. Then, more calmly, he said, 'It wouldn't do, Greg, can't you see? It would only alienate me further from the people I'm here to help if they were to see me living in comfort. And I don't fool myself—my living standards are already higher than anyone else's in San Stefano.'

'But not appreciably,' Claire remarked.

'You're not in a position to make that judgement as yet,' he rebuked her harshly. 'The only improvements I'd agree to would be those which would help medically. A generator, for example, would improve the surgery— with electricity, simple machinery could be installed. And a decent refrigerator would help, for drugs that have to be stored cold. Right now, I have this clapped-out old fridge that runs on bottled gas, but it's on its last legs, and carting the bottles up from Aguas is no joke.'

Darkness was falling rapidly, and they had eaten nothing since lunch, but Ashley seemed to have forgotten about such mundane trivialities.

'What else? Ah, yes—if we could have a proper well sunk, which would benefit the whole village. Clean, reliable water would be the greatest single health advantage anyone could provide.'

'I still think you have a duty to look after yourself,' Greg persisted. 'If you get sick, who's going to look after your patients? A few years like this could kill you—and I'm not joking.'

Ashley looked down at his hands clasped around the mug, and Claire saw a strange expression flit across his face, at the same time reminiscent and mutinous. An angry nostalgia.

'Not me, lad,' he said quietly. 'I grew up in a pit village, where bath night was a tin tub in front of the fire. My father was killed in a mining accident, but my mother wasn't the only young widow in the community, and we made do. I'm tougher than you think, and I'm used to making do.'

He rose abruptly, lit the kerosene lamp which swung from the ceiling, and strode across to the window.

'Here's Pilar, at last,' he said, and opened the door to admit a fat woman whose eyes were like jet beads in her puffy face, and whose breath came wheezingly. For all she had to struggle to get the words out, their flow never stopped, and although Claire could scarcely understand more than one word in ten, it was obviously a hard-luck story, full of excuses for her late appearance.

Ashley listened stonily, unimpressed.

'Pilar,' he said reprovingly, pointing to the floor and wrinkling his nose in disgust, *'está casa no está limpia. Y sucia—muy sucia!'*

The little black eyes glanced shiftily around the room, flitting uneasily over Basil and Greg, and resting a while longer on Claire, before Pilar burst into another spasm of explanation. Claire saw amusement twitching Ashley's lips as he ushered her unceremoniously into the kitchen, along with the basket of provisions she had brought with her.

'Did you catch any of that?' he demanded abruptly of Claire, and she shook her head.

'My understanding of Spanish is limited, and she went far too fast. But I'd have to be stupid not to grasp that some of it was about me, so you might as well tell me what the joke is,' she challenged.

'If you insist,' he agreed, and while his face was straight, his eyes were still laughing. 'She said she didn't know if I wanted her to cook and clean for me any more, now that I had brought my *mujer*—my woman—to San Stefano.'

Claire very nearly choked on her indignation.

'You mean—me?' she exclaimed, outraged. 'She thought that I was your...that's ridiculous!'

Basil's shoulders had begun to shake with the first humour he had displayed since his bottle of whisky had gone missing, and even Greg was chuckling slightly. This male conspiracy of amusement incensed Claire even further, and she rounded on them all, head high, shoulders braced.

'Oh, shut up, the lot of you! You're behaving like a gang of silly schoolboys, sniggering over a girly magazine!' she said disgustedly. Rounding on Ashley, she adopted the firm demeanour of a schoolmistress on the rampage. 'I just hope you made it clear to her that I was nothing of the kind!'

Ashley rubbed his jaw ruefully, as if she had slapped him.

'I did try, Claire, but I'm not too sure she swallowed my story, or that anyone else will. Glamorous young lady reporters are a bit thin on the ground in San Stefano, you see.'

'Don't be so patronising,' she said curtly. Without being sure why, she had a nagging suspicion that Ashley had not done all he should to remove any ambiguity about her status. He seemed to find a perverse satisfaction in causing her embarrassment. He had certainly lost no opportunity that arose to put her down since the first time they met. But, since she did not speak enough Spanish to know exactly what he *had* said, she was in no position to accuse him.

'Oh, come on, Claire,' Greg said, puzzled. 'Aren't you over-reacting a little? Where's your sense of humour all of a sudden?'

'Sure. It's no big deal what anyone thinks,' Basil agreed. 'So what?'

Nor was it, or course. This was a simple society, where every woman belonged to a man, in one sense or another. In other circumstances, Claire would have seen the funny side of the woman's mistake, and taken it in her stride.

No—she corrected herself, not in other circumstances, but if anyone other than Ashley Wade had been involved. Had Pilar assumed she was Greg Telford's woman, for instance, she would have been no more than mildly amused, understanding perfectly that single lady journalists from London were a little outside the scope of this rural, deeply conservative community, in its mountain fastness. She would not have taken umbrage so easily.

So why had she been so outraged when Pilar had assumed, not unnaturally, that the doctor was tired of living alone, and had brought along a woman from among his own kind, to alleviate his loneliness and see to his domestic needs? It did not require too much self-analysis to work out that it was the mere idea of Ashley and herself in a sexual situation that made her hot under the collar. Because she found the notion repugnant? Or because it held a secret fascination she did·not want to admit, even to herself?

Claire refused to proceed any further with these disturbing speculations. She had her hands full simply researching and writing her article, and it was juvenile to indulge in fantasies about a man she was not even sure she liked, although she grudgingly allowed that one had to admire what he was trying to do. If he felt any glimmer of respect for her, then all she could say was that he had hidden it very well indeed!

Dinner on that first night, when Pilar finally produced it, was some kind of stew composed primarily of maize with a few scrawny pieces of meat which looked as if it might once have been chicken...or there again, might not.

'It's best not to enquire too closely,' Ashley grinned, watching Greg poke around suspiciously with his fork. 'I can say this with impunity, since she doesn't speak any English—Pilar is a rotten cook. Her chief culinary tactic is to lace everything liberally with hot spices so it all tastes pretty much the same, and you stop worrying about whatever it is you're eating.'

Greg pushed his plate to one side.

'I seem to have lost my appetite,' he complained. 'If you don't mind...as you know, I had a bout of stomach trouble in Aguas Calientes, and I don't want to invite a recurrence.'

'No, I don't mind,' Ashley shrugged. 'But you're going to get damned hungry. There's not much variation on this theme. It's not entirely Pilar's fault. With what's available, the Roux brothers would have a hard time.'

'She doesn't look as if she fasts much herself,' Basil observed, forcing down a mouthful of the fiery concoction.

'Obesity, when you come across it in underdeveloped countries, isn't likely to be a result of over-indulgence,' Ashley said coolly. His glance sought Claire's face, challenging her to put her foot in things yet again, but here she felt more secure. This kind of dinner-time conversation took her back to the days when her father was still alive, reminding her of how he had liked to stimulate her interest in medical matters. Even now, her continued contact with specialists from different fields of medicine kept her informed on many related subjects.

'She probably has a glandular imbalance, which needs to be treated by replacing the missing hormones with a synthetic equivalent,' she said. 'I'm not going to guess which drug you're using, as there are several which are effective.'

'Who's a clever girl, then?' he said lightly. 'Actually, it's taken me the best part of a year to persuade her to give the treatment a chance. And I've had to be very careful in my choice of drug, since she has a tendency to angina.'

Claire glanced quickly into the kitchen, where Pilar was noisily stacking dirty dishes and pans.

'Pilar has heart trouble? Should she be doing your housework at all? Heaving baskets of food up that steep track, scrubbing floors...' she said indignantly.

'You think she'd be better off putting in seven days' a week hard labour in the fields, rather than cooking and cleaning for me?' he challenged. 'You've seen the state of this place. Believe me, she's not about to expire from over-exertion.'

His tone was caustically amused, and Claire saw then what should have been apparent to her before. He employed Pilar because she was otherwise unemployable. Unfit to undertake the punishing physical work on the land, she still was able to supplement her family's income by looking after the foreign doctor. So she wasn't an accomplished cook, and he could doubtless have found a younger, stronger woman who would have discharged her duties more efficiently. But this man did not think in the normal, logical, cost-effective manner which ran most of the world's affairs. Pilar was yet another beneficiary of the Ashley Wade Benevolent Society. He would never be rich. At this rate, he was unlikely even to be solvent. But who was to say he was wrong?

This disturbing revelation, which turned all accepted thinking upside-down, shook Claire to the roots of her complacency. She saw that she had done little more than skim the surface of life, and suddenly she saw cracks in the ice, perceived the dark waters beneath, and feared the unprepared plunge into its chilly depths.

'Excuse me!' she blurted out, jumping to her feet. 'I need some fresh air!' Stumbling to the door, she slipped out quickly, closing it behind her.

With darkness, the furnace-like heat had softened to a pleasant warmth, the hint of a breeze drifting down from the high mountains whose dark shapes brooded over the huddled village below. Cicadas whirred continuously, and one of the mules, disturbed by her presence, brayed from their enclosure. Claire took deep breaths, gulping in the welcome freshness, but she could not so easily dispel her confusion. She sighed and leaned on the fence, watching the animals imperturbably cropping the grass.

'Claire.'

She turned quickly. Ashley stood a little way from her, his arms folded, his face unreadable in the shadows. There was something unnerving about his stance and his manner which made her not merely reluctant, but actually afraid to be out here alone with him.

He caught her arm as she would have brushed past him, surprising her with the wiry strength of his grip.

'What is it with you?' he demanded.

Claire was totally unready for this kind of confrontation with him. Her own thoughts were still whirling around in her head; she needed to sort them out, marshal them into order, before she attempted to cross swords with him.

'I don't know what you mean,' she said icily.

'You know well enough. There's something about me that makes you uncomfortable. You think I'm crazy. You don't approve of my methods, you distrust my motives. All right. You don't have to like me—nor I, you—that isn't part of the deal, but both of us have a job to do. So get off my back, and let's get on with it.'

He still had hold of her arm, so tightly that Claire knew no amount of struggling would enable her to wrench herself free.

'The only thing about you that makes me uncomfortable is that you've done your best to embarrass and wrong-foot me from the moment we met!' she exploded furiously.

'Then you're easily embarrassed, lady! What I need is a fair-minded journalist who'll give a straight, unbiased report on my work, not a pampered female who gets the vapours if a man looks at her, and is repelled by the thought of a little hard work.'

'How dare you? That's not true at all!' Claire gasped indignantly.

'Isn't it? I suggest you take a hard look at your own life, and find out whatever it is that you lack,' he said harshly. 'In the meantime, kindly remember that I'm not responsible for it.'

'You are the rudest, most overbearing man I've ever had the misfortune to meet!' she cried. 'I can assure you, there's nothing lacking in my life—certainly nothing that *you* could provide!'

His fingers tightened still further, so that she had to suppress a desire to wince, pulling her closer.

'Sure about that, are you?' he asked, holding her like that for just a moment, before contemptuously letting her go.

CHAPTER FIVE

THE SLEEPING quarters of Ashley Wade's house were only marginally less primitive than camping. One climbed up a rough wooden ladder into a space beneath the roof, which was subdivided into two small, bare rooms, wooden-floored and furnished only with truckle beds. Claire had the smaller of these for herself, Greg and Basil shared the larger, and Ashley slept on the couch down below in the living area.

Only one small window admitted a minimum of light and air, and there were vague, unspecified scratchings and rustlings in the roof above. She had vague, unpleasant notions of rats jumping on her in the middle of the night, and she could hear Basil snoring loudly on the other side of the partition.

But even had she been tucked up cosily between cool cotton sheets, with room service a bell-push away, she would not have been able to sleep easily. It was impossible for her to suppress her raging indignation at Ashley's outspoken criticism, his rough handling and his totally unjustified insinuations.

She was prepared to admit that he annoyed her, that she had been unable to resist the occasional dig at him, and their conversation frequently degenerated into argument. But he was as much to blame for that as she. Everything about her was wrong in his eyes: what she said, how she behaved, even how she looked, and he seized on every chance to point this out.

Claire tossed restlessly, unable to shut out the memory of his hard grip on her arm, and his words—'take a long, hard look at your life, and find out what it is that you lack.' There was just enough truth in them to echo thoughts that had been troubling her, she was honest enough not to deny that. But what had her simmering with indignation was his hinting accusation that frustration was at the root of this void in her life, and that he might hold the cure for it.

I'm not attracted to him—not in the least, she insisted firmly, closing her eyes and trying to blot out the day's tribulations. She would be good for nothing unless she got some sleep.

When she did finally drift off, it seemed to be for no more than a moment, and then it was morning again. The brilliant, already hot sun streamed through the tiny window, turning her 'bedroom' into a stifling oven, and she could hear movement beyond the partition.

Feeling drugged and heavy-eyed, she rummaged in her bag for a brush, dragged it through her hair and tied it hurriedly with a ribbon, before scrambling into jeans and a half-way clean shirt.

There was no one in the living-room when she scrambled down the ladder in the least ungainly manner she could manage, but the door stood open and the blanket had been thrown back over the couch, so obviously Ashley was up and about somewhere. The stove was already hot and glowing, and Claire thought longingly of crisp bacon and succulent sausage, grilled mushrooms and tomatoes—a breakfast she was certainly not going to get, she told herself with a rueful grin.

A curiosity she could not resist made her turn to Ashley's home-made bookshelves. The contents were not volumes of medical reference—those, presumably, he kept in the surgery—but personal reading matter. A wide choice of novels, from D. H. Lawrence to Dick Francis,

all in well-thumbed paperback. The odd atlas, encyclo-
paedia, and several travelogues, all about relatively civilised areas like the Camargue, or the Italian Lakes—good
escapist stuff for a rural medic stuck in the third world
back of beyond. And, most surprisingly, volume after
volume of poetry—Wordsworth, Hopkins, Yeats, Sylvia
Plath—the list went on.

Idly, Claire picked up a volume of Coleridge, and by
one of those incredible coincidences—or maybe the
owner liked the poem, and the page opened there from
long habit—she found herself reading the very lines
which had eluded her yesterday.

'In Xanadu did Kubla Khan
A stately pleasure-dome decree;
Where Alph, the sacred river, ran
Through caverns measureless to man
Down to a sunless sea.'

He startled her, coming in with the bucket of water
from the well, and she almost dropped the book, closing
it hastily. She felt absurdly like a guilty first year
schoolgirl, caught in the sixth-form common-room.

'Feel free to plunder the library, by all means, but in
your spare time,' he remarked pointedly.

'Sorry,' Claire retorted, the ready gorge of irritation
making her rise predictably to take the bait. 'I wasn't
aware I was shirking any of my duties right now. Perhaps
you should post up a rota.'

'That's an idea,' he agreed unworriedly. An oddly
boyish grin spread across the lean face, reminding her
that he really was a very young man to have taken on
so much heavy responsibility, roughly the same age as
the young men she knew in London, who chatted up
girls in wine bars, after a day spent shifting paper in
offices—or planning campaigns to make people spend

money on luxury merchandise they didn't really need, she thought, a sudden, unwelcome image of Jon springing into her mind.

'I hate to interrupt your reveries,' Ashley said, handing her a raffia basket, 'but if you really want breakfast, I suggest you go see if the chickens have obliged us this morning.'

'I didn't know you kept chickens,' Claire said, surprise diverting her from the barb in his words.

'You didn't know I liked poetry, either,' he observed. 'How could a rough Yorkshireman from a mining village appreciate the refinements of Shelley and Dryden? It must be difficult for a Sloane Ranger like yourself to understand that there's life and intelligence north of Watford.'

Claire all but exploded.

'*Sloane Ranger?* I'll have you know I'm a country doctor's daughter from Sussex!' she told him sharply. 'I earn my own living because I *have* to, I'm not filling in time between finishing school and marriage! You should do something about that outsize chip on your shoulder, Dr Wade!'

She stomped off outside in a fine old temper, but it must have been something to do with the soothing, healing powers of nature, for five minutes with the soft, feathery warmth of the clucking chickens, and the satisfaction of seeing the raffia basket fill up, made it impossible for her to remain angry. She could even see the funny side of being mistaken for one those rangy, well-dressed hooray-Henriettas who strode loud-voiced through Harrods!

'The hens have been good to you today,' she told him, returning to the welcome smell of coffee brewing. 'I see you're trying to grow vegetables out there, too.'

'"Trying" being the operative word,' he said ruefully. 'The soil is pathetically poor, and I don't really give it as much attention as I should.'

Claire wondered faintly how he found the time and energy at all, but the appearance of Greg and Basil prevented her from developing this line of thought any further.

Claire could see that what worried Greg most was the non-existent wardrobe facilities which made it impossible to maintain a fine crease in his trousers. Basil was unusually taciturn. He'd been more than two days without a drink, and there was an edgy, dangerous gleam in his eyes which made Claire uneasy.

'It looks as if Pilar isn't going to turn up early enough to do breakfast today,' Ashley said philosophically. 'We'll have to fend for ourselves. We have bread, eggs and coffee. Pilar makes a kind of tortilla—a cross between a pancake and an omelette—which I can roughly approximate. I must admit, I hanker for really fluffy scrambled eggs, but that's a knack I don't have.'

'And I thought, from what you said on the trek up, that you were a master chef,' Claire could not resist saying. 'There's nothing to it, if you beat the eggs hard enough and get the fat really hot.'

He sketched a brief bow and handed her the pan.

'I'm always willing to defer to an expert,' he called her bluff quickly.

There was nothing for it but to proceed, fearful that if in this strange, primitive kitchen, the skill she had deserted her, the egg would be on her face! But, surprisingly, she found she could produce as good results with the iron pan over the open coals as she did on her electric hob at home. The eggs were delicious, and even Basil, who was not usually fit to face food before midday, ate and enjoyed breakfast.

'I have to make it clear I'm not scrubbing the pan,' Claire announced firmly. 'Pilar can do that, when she does turn up.'

After they had eaten, Ashley, with the first diffidence he had so far shown, asked Claire if she would like to sit in on his 'surgery,' while Greg investigated the state of the pharmacological supplies to ascertain what the doctor was using, what he lacked, and how the situation could be improved on. She agreed willingly. Here, at last, she could see the start of what she had come to Rio Negro to do, and all the petty frustrations and irritations fell away from her as her mental muscles flexed in readiness.

Basil announced his intention of prowling around to get some general background shots, and insisted on doing this alone, in spite of Ashley's doubts about the advisability of this course.

'I always work alone—I can't take shots with anyone breathing down my back,' he insisted. 'I've worked in out of the way places before, and I'll be discreet about filming. You don't need to worry.'

Claire got her notebook, pens and tape recorder, and Ashley opened up the adjoining rooms he used to see and treat his patients. Greg went straight into the storeroom, where the shelves of medication and other supplies were kept.

In many ways, Claire thought, there were similarities with GPs' surgeries everywhere: the shelves of medical reference works, the everyday equipment of a doctor's craft. But the resemblance was incomplete. Here, there was no up-to-date equipment and very little modern technology. Ashley Wade had had to start from scratch and provide everything without any public backing, and everything he had was clearly well used and at least second-hand.

Claire was surprised by a fierce pang of sympathetic admiration as she looked around at the home-made shelves, the rough wooden desk and couch, the well-worn equipment.

'I'd say you could do with a new microscope, doctor,' she said gently. 'I haven't seen one like that for years.'

'Most of this stuff I acquired from friends and contacts who were in the process of pensioning it off,' he admitted. 'It's not ideal, and there's always the worry that something vital may give up on me at any time. But beggars can't be choosers.'

He straightened his shoulders, deliberately replacing despair with a jaunty, cheerful pragmatism.

'We'd best make a start. I've been away for quite a few days, so there will be a fair-sized queue.' He opened the door. 'As you see, we don't have refinements like waiting-rooms.'

Claire saw. Her eyes opened wider as she took in the long line of patiently waiting humanity outside. She had not known they were there at all, because for the most part they were so quiet—an unnatural, suffering, passive silence that did not really expect its ills to be relieved or its lot to improve in any essential respect. Here and there a child cried, and was hushed, but that was all. Blank, dark eyes stared at her from lined, weatherbeaten faces, full of stark endurance. A 'narcosis of despair', Ashley had called it, and she knew now exactly what he had meant by those words. Squatting cross-legged on the floor, leaning against the wall as if today, tomorrow, or next year were all the same, nursing its thin, undernourished children, the populace of San Stefano and beyond waited resignedly for the attention of one lean, rude, angry and utterly dedicated young Yorkshireman whom it very probably failed to appreciate.

'Let's be having you,' Ashley Wade muttered under his breath, and held open the door for the first of the long stream of patients, a young man of twenty-five, according to Ashley's records, although he looked much older to Claire, as did all the local people. He had a nasty-looking tropical ulcer on his leg, an area of fluid-filled blebs which had begun to break down into a foul-smelling grey mass.

Claire shuddered with a sympathy he at once mistook for mere distaste.

'There's no need to wrinkle your nose yet. This is one of the less severe cases,' he told her sternly. 'I'm trying to persuade people to seek treatment before these things, which are common in poor, agricultural communities, reach a stage where all sorts of complications can set in. More often than not they resort to homespun remedies which would make your hair curl. Pass me the gauze . . . no, over there, on the table . . . and hydrogen peroxide to clean it out . . .'

Claire was about to protest that it was difficult to take notes and observe, while labouring for him at the same time. But he *was* single-handed, and there *was* a long queue waiting outside, so she did his bidding without demur. And so it went on. Appalled and depressed, Claire lost count of the number and variety of ailments the peasants of San Stefano were heir to, the different kinds of skin disease, the worms and parasites, the almost monotonous recurrence of intestinal complains, and the all too common nutritional disease, particularly and distressingly in young children.

And Ashley Wade did not play fair. Not content with her constantly taking notes and struggling to understand complaint, diagnosis and treatment, he used her mercilessly as a kind of surrogate nurse, demanding as of right that she fetch and carry bowls and instruments, run to Greg for various medications, help bandage, soothe, and administer comfort.

She bit her lip to repress her anguish at so much suffering, and he glanced up, misreading her expression.

'Don't pull such a face. These are only the walking wounded,' he said reprovingly.

"I wasn't . . .' she began, and then gave up with a sigh. This wasn't the time to explain how all this affected her. 'I'm not a nurse, Ashley,' she reminded him quietly.

'Good grief! Anyone can unwind bandages and throw away soiled dressings,' he said impatiently, and turned his back on her to explain patiently, slowly, and with due respect to the language barrier which sometimes still perplexed him, why wearing shoes around the house would help his patient avoid a recurrence of hookworm.

'I hear myself saying these things to people, and I don't wonder they look at me as if I'm the one who needs treatment,' he said scornfully. 'She probably only has one pair of shoes, and isn't going to wear them out indoors, where barefoot will do. I rattle on about hygiene in a place with no running water or proper sewage disposal! Better conditions would put half of these bugs out of business, but damn it, I can't prescribe them!'

'Can I quote those words exactly?' Claire asked quietly.

'Quote what the hell you like,' he replied tersely. 'I very rarely say anything I don't mean and am not prepared to repeat.'

Claire was about to retort angrily that none of this was her fault, and being rude to her would resolve little. But a dawning understanding stilled her tongue. His anger was not directed at her, but at forces and circumstances he was powerless to influence, and throughout the long session, fraught with difficulties and frustrations, he had kept it, for the most part, admirably under control. With his patients, most of whom were near-illiterate and full of suspicion, he was laconically courteous, and although Claire couldn't see his bedside manner going down too well in any of the snobbier new private hospitals springing up back home, there was no doubting his concern or his commitment. She could feel it, and she was sure that on some level, these people were able to feel it, too, in spite of the vast chasm of culture and upbringing separating them.

She was fighting hard to control the heart-wrenching pity that made tears threaten to well up in her eyes as another pot-bellied, stick-legged infant was carried into the surgery. What use was too-easy sentimentality? she asked herself...and he would probably despise her for it. The child had a nasty scorpion sting on his foot, he was in a lot of pain, and his mother was almost as scared as he was. Without thinking, Claire lifted him on to her lap—he was so light it involved no effort—and held his hand while Ashley administered an injection.

'That didn't hurt, did it?' he asked, and since he spoke in English, she presumed the question was directed at her rather than the patient.

They worked well into the afternoon, without so much as a breath of air or a cup of coffee. Claire was exhausted, and only a dogged insistence that she would keep going as long as he did kept her functioning. In the normal course of her work, she came up against illness frequently, but only as an observer. She had never been on the front line, as she was today, and, in addition to all she was called on to do, she had to fight hard to hold at bay that visceral reaction of fear and revulsion which took her back to...to that long ago day she preferred not to think of.

That she managed to do so surprised her, and she admitted to herself that she owed much to the matter-of-fact calmness of Ashley Wade, who accepted that the enemy was stronger than he was, and fought it nevertheless. But she did not dare ask herself how well this fragile endurance would serve her if she came slap up against something traumatically horrifying.

At last the queue of patients came to an end. Greg had taken his leave of them long ago, and Claire could not hide her fatigue as she looked at Ashley.

'You really do need a nurse,' she suggested. 'Couldn't you get a local girl who knows and understands the problems?'

'It's a pipe dream, I'm afraid,' he said. 'Trained nurses are hard to come by, even in the cities where the big hospitals are. It's a badly paid, low-status profession in this country, and few Rio Negran girls would jump at the chance to work here, in conditions those with any education have fought hard to escape from. Nor could I afford to pay one.'

Claire smiled grimly.

'Then the only way you could do it would be to take some home leave, and lure one from the clutches of the NHS by marrying her,' she said lightly.

It was said in jest, as she expected it to be taken, but Claire was surprised by the sudden darkening of his expression. The deep blue eyes regarded her with cold hostility, and his humorous mouth hardened as he drew his lips tightly together, leaving her in no doubt that she had unwittingly said something he found offensive.

She held up her hand in a gesture of apology.

'Joke,' she said wryly.

'It was in poor taste, then,' he replied curtly. Claire stared at him. It had been a harmless enough remark, said facetiously, it was true, but surely there was nothing in it to evoke such outrage? Once again, it appeared, she had angered him, and this time, not only had it been quite unintentional, but she hadn't a hope of knowing why. And she had no wish to drive herself deeper into the mire of misunderstanding by seeking an explanation. If the subject was touchy, it was best dropped.

'If that's the last of the patients, can we close up?' she asked quietly. 'Greg finished checking the stores some time ago, and I'm anxious to see if Basil got his shots.'

Together they emerged into the blinding, enervating heat of the afternoon, and walked back to the house in silence.

She was glad of Greg's presence, and hoped she could absent herself while the two men discussed the relative merits of various drugs, and the state of Ashley's supplies. But the usually suave executive wore a troubled expression, owing to the fact that Basil had gone missing.

Claire frowned.

'He's a perfectionist in his work, and he'll spend ages getting the light, the angle, everything just as he wants it,' she said. 'But all the same . . . where can he have got to?'

'Not taking photographs, that's for sure,' Greg said grimly. 'His equipment is all upstairs, and from what I can gather from Pilar, he came back some time ago and went out again. Does that suggest anything to you?'

'It suggests to me that after two days of total abstinence, he's in search of something to drink,' Claire stated baldly. She stole a sidelong glance at Ashley, whose expression clearly said 'I told you so', although he refrained from comment. 'All right, so we shouldn't have left him alone so long. But how was I to know morning surgery would last until tea time?' she added defensively.

'This is San Stefano, lass, not Esher,' Ashley said cryptically. Her cheeks stung from the reproof, but surprisingly, he took some of the sting out of it by adding, 'I'm the one to blame. I should have followed my own

judgement, which was not to let him out of my sight.
He's a whisker away from being an alcoholic, and
whoever chose him for this assignment needs a brain
transplant! I'd better go find him before he lands himself
in real trouble.'

'I'll come with you,' Greg volunteered at once, but
Ashley shook his head.

'Thanks for the offer, but best not. I know these
people, and you don't. They'll tolerate my in-
trusion...just.' He sketched a grin. 'Tell Pilar to make
some coffee...lots of it.'

He was out the door and away down the track before
either of them could say another word of protest, and
they looked at one another helplessly.

'He's probably right,' Claire said consolingly. 'He does
know the village, and people are used to seeing him
around. Hopefully, Basil won't cause any trouble. He's
not aggressive when he's drinking. Usually he gets very
cheerful, and then falls asleep.'

She ventured into the kitchen and tried to convey her
needs to Pilar.

'*Señora...café solo...mucho, por favor,*' she es-
sayed politely.

Pilar grunted something which might or might not
have been consent, glowering suspiciously at Claire as
she poured water into the pan. It was difficult to make
friends with the woman, who continued to see Claire as
a threat to her own position. Even had her command of
Spanish been up to it—which it decidedly was not—
Claire would hardly have known how to express, deli-
cately, that Pilar was in no danger of being usurped,
that she herself was not, in any sense of the word, Ashley
Wade's 'woman'. Perish the thought, she reflected
angrily.

For the next half-hour she waited with increasing anxiety for Ashley to reappear, bringing Basil back to safety. Her worries on behalf of the photographer were easy to explain away. He was a colleague whom she had known, if only casually, for some years, and he was a stranger to this part of the world. But a part of herself which she resented, yet could not suppress, was troubled for the safety of the ill-mannered doctor. She could not help remembering all those closed, sullen expressions as they passed through the village, and, although she did not particularly admire herself for harbouring such un-charitable suspicions, well…he *was* a foreigner, a *gringo*, and people could be unpredictable. The fact that he rep-resented the only medical help for miles around, and that the same people queued hours to see him, did not automatically guarantee that he would come to no harm.

'Why should I care?' she asked herself irritably, but she was shocked by the wave of relief which swept over her as she saw Ashley struggling up the path, supporting Basil, who was barely on his feet, head drooping, legs dragging. She ran swiftly down the path towards them.

'Thank goodness you're back!'

'Worried about me, were you?' he quipped lightly, raising sardonic eyebrows. 'I never knew you cared.'

'I don't!' she flashed back. 'But I've enough sense to know we'd be in a pretty pickle here without you. And I had good reason to be worried about Basil—he looks half-dead!'

Greg joined them, and together he and Ashley carried the almost unconscious photographer inside and laid him on the couch. His breathing was ragged and uneven, his face deathly white with a tinge of green. Even Claire had never seen him like this before.

'He sniffed out the *cantina*, and was heavily into the local moonshine,' Ashley said grimly. Forcing Basil into a half sitting position, he shouted for Pilar to bring cold water, hot coffee, and a bucket, in that order.

'Is it necessary to be quite so unfeeling?' Claire demanded, horrified. 'He'll sleep it off, if left alone.'

'That rotgut at the *cantina* isn't exactly finest malt whisky,' Ashley said abruptly. 'I wasn't joking when I said it could be lethal. We have to get some of it out of his system, or there's a real danger of alcoholic poisoning.'

He doused Basil's face with cold water, and the photographer sputtered indignantly and began to cough.

'That's better, lad,' Ashley said, quite gently, supporting his shoulders to prevent him flopping back on the couch. He turned to Claire. 'Now we'll use the time-honoured method of making him vomit. Enough of Pilar's coffee should do the trick.'

It did. Copious quantities of the thick, black, unsweetened brew were forced down Basil's throat, until his stomach revolted against the treatment, and he was violently sick.

'Hence the bucket,' Ashley said calmly. Claire found herself mopping Basil's brow and cleaning his face with a damp cloth, without the doctor's having to ask for her help. Some instinct she had not known she possessed simply took over.

All three of them were glad to step outside for a breath of fresh air, leaving Basil snoring on the couch.

'I'll say one thing, Ashley—so far, this visit had been an experience I'm unlikely to forget,' Greg said with feeling. His usually immaculately brushed hair was ruffled, his shirt and trousers none too clean, but astonishingly, he was smiling. They had been in San Stefano only just over a day, and already it had begun to change them in a subtle, indefinable way.

'You're welcome,' Ashley grinned back. 'Beats the average package tour into a cocked hat, doesn't it?'

Greg actually laughed as he strolled over to talk to the mules, for whom he had discovered a reluctant fondness.

'How about you, Claire?' Ashley interrogated quietly. 'Would you say the same? Have you derived any benefit from being here, or it it just an unpleasant episode you'll be glad to put behind you?'

He was referring, she knew, to those unquantifiable inner changes on which she had just been musing, and she hesitated, unsure of how to answer. This morning, she had begun to see San Stefano not just as a spot on the map in a deprived, third-world country, but in terms of real people, with families and lives, and problems which needed help in the solving. She'd overcome a little of the fear of being involved with suffering. And she had come closer to understanding and appreciating the urge which drove this man to pit himself against such terrifying odds.

What troubled her was how to put any of this into words without giving away too much of her own secret self, and as she struggled inwardly with her conflict, he mistook the nature of her silence.

'Silly of me. I don't expect it's ever occurred to you for one minute that you might have anything to learn,' he said scathingly, and, turning his back on her, he disappeared into the house.

CHAPTER SIX

BASIL, after sleeping through until morning, woke up with the worst hangover he had ever had in his life.

'Am I going to die?' he asked, flopping back on the couch where he had spent the night. 'I guess it might be a relief. Go on, say it!' He looked sourly at Ashley, who regarded him with non-committal blankness. 'I guess you have the right. You *did* warn me.' And I should have known that anything that smelled and probably tasted like antifreeze would be rough on the stomach.'

Ashley shrugged.

'I tried it myself, when I first came here. I'm not averse to the odd pint of beer in the pub back home, and I can appreciate a glass of good brandy. But I soon decided it wasn't worth it.'

Basil managed a painful smile, and eyed the doctor with new understanding. The approach, Claire observed with surprised admiration, was not teacher to pupil, or preacher to sinner, but man to man.

'I must have passed out,' he said. 'I can't recall you coming into the *cantina*, or how I got back here...but I remember the expressions on the faces of the men in that place...or rather, the lack of expression! They looked like robots! Man, I don't ever want to get like that!'

Ashley did not labour the point, since Basil had grasped it well enough for himself.

'You won't be feeling much like breakfast, I take it?' he grinned, and Basil pulled a face.

'Spare me!' he muttered. Dragging himself to his feet, he hauled himself up the ladder to the sleeping quarters, away from the aroma of greasy frying which usually attended whatever Pilar produced in the kitchen.

But today it was not Pilar who appeared, but a much younger woman, little more than a girl, slim and sloe-eyed, who walked with an undulating grace. She could not have been older than sixteen, for the familiar hangdog look of poverty had not yet snuffed out the bright flame of youth. Her hips and breasts were nicely rounded, she had all her teeth—very white ones, too—and rich black hair rippled to her shoulders. Given a few years of marriage, frequent childbirth, and want, she could very swiftly become a wizened crone of indeterminate age, but as of now she was desirable, and very much aware of it.

The thick, dark lashes veiled her eyes with oblique coyness as she talked to Ashley, standing closer to him than was necessary, Claire thought, since the man wasn't deaf. He smiled down at her with brotherly indulgence, and she returned the smile with one of limpid invitation before slinking gracefully into the kitchen.

'Who's the raven-haired siren?' Greg asked, with faintly raised eyebrows.

'That's Yolanda, Pilar's eldest daughter,' Ashley said. 'Pilar isn't well enough to come today, and when that's the case, she sends Yolanda along instead. I'll look in at their place later to see how she is.'

'Let's hope Yolanda is a better cook than her mother,' Greg said feelingly, but Ashley laughed, shaking his head.

'That's a vain hope, I'm afraid. Mama must have taught them all the same way. Perhaps Claire would like to demonstrate to Yolanda how eggs should be cooked.'

'Uh-uh!' Claire attempted to disregard his amusement, but the familiar annoyance began to rise within her. 'It's bad enough getting black looks from Pilar. I don't intend to tangle with Carmen Miranda in there!'

Ashley's alert blue eyes continued to regard her with quizzical humour.

'You must know that Pilar doesn't dislike you personally,' he said loftily. 'She's only frightened of possible competition.'

'And Yolanda might be even more frightened!' Claire responded tartly. 'If the way she looked at you is any indication, it's a wonder she hasn't already moved in!'

The humour vanished from his eyes.

'Now you're being absurd!' he rapped. 'The girl is only fifteen, and while I'm not quite old enough to be her father, cradle-snatching doesn't appeal to me. Besides, I'm not...

'Interested in women?' Claire filled in sweetly, an uncharitable but highly pleasant satisfaction coursing through her. 'A joke is one thing if *I'm* the butt of it, isn't it, Ashley? I'm supposed to grin and bear it, right? But it's a different kettle of fish if *you're* at the receiving end!'

A vein throbbed near his temple, his hands clenched fiercely, and he looked angry enough to throttle her. Alarm leapt briefly in Claire's breast, and then the storm passed, and he was calm again.

'OK. We don't need this kind of hassle,' he conceded tersely. 'We have a hard enough job to accomplish, even if we all pull together. I promise to lay off sexist jokes, if you'll do the same.'

Greg intervened placatingly, the manager in him coming to the forefront.

'Ashley, since this business about Pilar seems to bother Claire, why don't you just explain to her that Claire has a regular *"hombre"* back home?' he suggested. 'That would set her mind at rest, and the atmosphere would be a whole lot easier.'

Ashley surveyed Claire with a critical interest which made her feel like a dead insect under a slide.

'Is that a fact?' There was a lurking amusement she did not like, just beneath the level surface of his voice. 'I wasn't aware you were what my mother used to call "spoken for".'

Claire squirmed a little. She had told Greg she was involved with someone simply to nip in the bud any attraction he might show signs of developing, and now her words had rebounded on her. It had been partly fiction when she'd said it, and now it was wholly untrue. She had scarcely thought of Jon since she'd arrived in Rio Negro, and every instinct told her that she could never go back to him. She was no longer the woman who had accepted his comings and goings, his easy, inconsequential approach to life. Rio Negro and Ashley Wade between them had seen to that.

'There's no reason why you should have known, since my private life is my own business,' she retorted. That was true, but a small voice inside her insisted that it might be better if she preserved this useful fiction. It would serve to keep a distance between herself and this man who alternately infuriated and mystified her, so she did not deny it.

'Hm.' Ashley's voice was thoughtful. 'What does your...er...friend think about your disappearing off on missions to dangerous out-of-the-way places? I'd be perturbed, to say the least, if you were my lady.'

'Fortunately, I'm not your lady,' Claire snapped back, quite tartly. 'I'm simply doing my job. That's all there is to it.'

Jon, actually, had been rather miffed about Claire's going 'up the Amazon without a paddle' as he put it. She had been well aware that his displeasure did not stem from concern for her safety, but a jealous pique that her career seemed to be taking off, while his own stagnated. She got a hazardous but prestigious assignment to Central America, and he was stuck producing washing-powder commercials in deepest Hendon!

She wasn't about to tell Ashley Wade about the ensuing unpleasantness which had ended with a noisy party in her flat, to which she wasn't invited, and a bathroom sink clogged with long red hairs! Her chin went up, and she stared at him challengingly, daring him to pass any further comment on her supposedly loving relationship with another man.

But Ashley, whatever his deficiencies, was not short on nerve.

'You'll have to excuse my somewhat old-fashioned attitude,' he said, without a trace of apology in his voice. 'Where I come from, men tend to have a more proprietary interest in their womenfolk. The permissive society hadn't really arrived when I left, and I haven't had time to catch up with it since.'

Greg, alarmed by the Pandora's box of emotions he had unwittingly opened, tried to disperse the tension with humour.

'Come off it, Ashley,' he laughed. 'You aren't that old, and Yorkshire isn't that backward, I'm sure!'

Ashley's features hardened into a touchy defensiveness.

'I'm twenty-nine, and I never said it was backward,' he declared. 'There's a harder, simpler, more realistic outlook on life once you get north of the Trent. Living together and leading separate lives still isn't considered trendy. It's called "living over t'brush" and that's not a compliment.'

Surprisingly, he laughed, a short, oddly diffident expression of amusement, turned inward upon himself.

'I'm the victim of a stern northern upbringing which I can't quite shake off,' he confessed wryly.

As they sat down to breakfast, Claire was plagued by the feeling that he disapproved of her... that that stern northern upbringing caused him to see her as lax and immoral, a product of a sexually relaxed London lifestyle where people changed partners with easy regularity.

But in her case it was far from true. There had been one brief, passionate teenage romance when youth and ignorance had combined to convince her she was madly in love. That experience had scalded her badly, and she had steered clear of serious involvement for a long time, restricting herself to friendship and 'dates'. Then there had been Jon. He was unfairly good-looking, charming, and, in the beginning, fun to be with. One night, relaxed after a good meal and rather more wine than she usually drank, she had allowed romance to spill over into something more serious.

She had been ready for... she wasn't sure what, and she recognised now that she had not really found it. Making love was enjoyable enough, but in no way the earth-shattering event poetry and literature had led her to believe it could be. And her life story was hardly a saga of permissive abandon, for a woman of twenty-four, in the second half of the twentieth century. Ashley had branded her, unfairly, with an image she did not merit.

Why should she care? she asked herself aggrievedly. But it wasn't any use protesting that her life was her own, and one man's opinion did not concern her. She *did* care about being wrongly labelled by him, and in a brief, private moment she tried to remedy this.

'Ashley, I think you might have got the wrong idea about Jon and me,' she said in a low voice. 'We aren't exactly living together in the way you meant. That is to say, he has his own place, and I have mine.'

'Claire.' The blue eyes were disconcertingly direct. 'As you yourself pointed out, your sex-life is no business of mine. You've probably realised that I tend to speak first and think afterwards.' He tapped his nose. '"Keep *that* out" was another of my mother's aphorisms. I'll try to follow it.'

'Your mother sounds like a remarkable woman,' she observed. 'You quote her all the time.'

'She's dead,' he said shortly, the frown shadowing his forehead caused not by disapproval, this time, but by genuine pain. His reply was so bleak and unadorned that Claire sucked in her breath and could not find anything to say. All the commonplace expressions of regret sounded like trite platitudes in the face of such deeply felt grief, and although she sensed him waiting for a response, she was unable to produce one, aware that the longer her silence lasted, the more it resembled coldness.

'It's not an uncommon story,' he said bluntly, after a while. 'I was twelve when my father was killed down the pit. I'd just got a scholarship to the best local grammar school, and my mother was determined I was going to stay there until I passed my A-levels. No son of hers was going down the mine, she was quite adamant. It was a struggle. There weren't many jobs for a woman in her middle years, without too much education. Cleaning, working behind bars in pubs, washing up in cafés—she did them all, often at the same time. I did paper rounds and holiday jobs, but she wouldn't let me help out too much, because of all the homework. "Get your head screwed on right, lad,'' she used to say. "Get yourself out of here, and don't come back.'' So to medical college I went, expecting to emerge as the great provider. But she didn't last six months after I took my finals.'

The bleakness was back, and impulsively Claire put a hand on top of his, where it rested on the rough table.

'But she knew you had succeeded in what you set out to do,' she said. 'That must have given her immense satisfaction.'

Unwillingly, she thought of her own father, who would have given much to see his daughter with MD after her name, but had been denied the pleasure. And she, Claire, did not have the excuse of shortage of cash and deprived circumstances. They were comfortably off, and it was not necessary for her to leave school to augment the family income. Yet this miner's widow's son had made it, through hard work, backed by parental single-mindedness and sheer guts. Whereas I, she thought soberly, just did not have what it took.

She'd forgotten that her hand was still resting on his until, looking down, she was startled by the contrast between them—hers, in spite of her skin's recent exposure to strong sunlight, was only the colour of pale honey against the sun-weathered darkness of his. The sinews stood out strongly, emphasising the slim femininity of her hand with its oval-tipped nails.

He turned it over and, still holding it in a firm grip, studied the vulnerable white palm, his thumb grazing gently over the fleshy pad below hers. Claire had never felt so weak, so helpless, and at the same time so fiercely and vibrantly female. She gasped and snatched her hand away, as if she had burned it.

'All right, Ms Mallory—I only held your hand, and *he* won't know about it,' he said amusedly. 'Back to business. How would you like to do a "round" with me? I warn you, it won't be the most pleasurable experience you've ever had.'

'So long as you don't ask me to help you remove an appendix, or anything like that,' she said, only half joking.

'Only in the direst of emergencies,' promised Ashley Wade, and she had the uncomfortable feeling that *he* was only half joking, too.

In the relative cool of the evening, Claire leaned on the fence, watching the grazing mules, and relishing the refreshing breeze which lifted the hair at the nape of her neck. A brilliant moon sailed high above the dark mountains, and in its cleansing brightness the houses of San Stefano below looked white and picturesque.

Having spent the best part of the day with Ashley, visiting those too sick to struggle to the surgery, Claire knew that this was an illusion. Their homes were for the most part dark and insanitary, poorly furnished and devoid of what she considered the basics of living—fresh running water, electricity and plumbing. In short, they were little more than hovels, even where she could see that the occupants were waging a desperate battle to live with a minimum of decency and cleanliness. No wonder people became ill in such conditions, she thought indignantly, infected by some of the driving anger which fuelled her companion. How could the despotic bureaucracy back in the capital maintain there was no need for a doctor in vast, backward rural areas such as this? When she finally wrote her article for *World Focus*, there was going to be no mincing of words, she decided grimly.

'Proper housing, clean water and the efficient use of insecticides would go a long way to reducing the incidence of disease,' he agreed readily, but when Claire pointed out that there weren't enough hours in the day for him to be environmental health officer, as well as doctor, for the entire area, his mouth tightened stubbornly, and he refused to discuss it further.

In spite of all the poverty and deprivation she saw at close quarters, and the truly fearful range of diseases Ashley was attempting to diagnose and treat, the worst moment for Claire was when they called to check a patient recovering from hepatitis, and discovered two children of the same family showing the distinctive rash of measles.

The children, Fernando and Anita, not more than a year apart in age, looked very sick and distressed, and Claire was stricken to learn that this common childhood ailment was, here, one of the prime causes of child mortality. Holding the little girl in her arms, she was stricken to think that she might die, and there was little, medically, that could be done to help.

'It's a virus, Claire, and there's no drug which can influence it,' he told her. 'Yes, I know there's a vaccine available, and I want to get a full programme of vaccination off the ground—polio, TAB, BCG—the lot. But there's the expense, and all the practical difficulties. I'll bet you thought tuberculosis was only encountered in Victorian novels, but it's a killer here, Ms Mallory.'

Claire was still trembling with distress over the two children with measles.

'I wish you'd stop calling me that!' she burst out fiercely.

'It's merely out of deference to your liberated status,' he replied, straight-faced.

'I am *not* liberated!' Claire exclaimed exasperatedly, and then went on, flustered, 'Well, yes, I *am*, but not in the way that you mean!'

'You're trying to tell me that you're just a sweet, old-fashioned girl at heart?' he grinned.

'Oh, shut up!' she exclaimed helplessly. How could he indulge in this intermittent flow of bantering humour, in the midst of all this hardship and sickness? she wondered.

Only now, standing in the moonlight, in a more reflective mood, did it occur to her that the banter and the jesting were probably his way of dealing with the endless suffering he was obliged to witness, and furthermore, it was probably what had helped support her through the day. Constantly stimulated by irritation and annoyance, she had not given way, she had kept going... and survived.

She had cut and folded bandages, helped with dressings, measured doses, held hands and murmured words of comfort that could be readily understood, even in a foreign tongue. And the lifelong fear had receded to a safe distance, from where she could confront it without going to pieces. Today, her tentative new courage had taken a further small step forward.

'All right?'

His quiet voice behind her made her spin round quickly, and she felt her heartbeat quicken unreasonably.

'Yes. I just needed to be out in the open for a spell, while it's cool enough. How's Greg?'

'Asleep. He and Basil make a pretty picture.'

They had arrived home from the village to find that Greg had abandoned his report, and was knocking the daylights out of Ashley's struggling vegetable patch with a spade and hoe. His once immaculate jeans were filthy, he was red and perspiring, and full of a boyish satisfaction.

'Your soil needed turning, and it was baked as hard as iron,' he said. 'You need some good fertiliser on this lot, Ashley, if you're to have any hopes at all. I'll do some soil analysis, and see what we can come up with.'

Then he had gasped, staggered indoors, and collapsed with heat exhaustion. Ashley had berated him soundly for indulging in such hard physical effort in the heat of the day, taken his pulse and temperature, and prescribed rest and fluid.

'You must find us a fine collection of greenhorns,' Claire said wryly.

She sensed him smiling in the darkness, and for once his laughter was not derisive.

'I was a greenhorn myself when I first came here,' he admitted. 'You could have filled a book with the things I didn't know. But this is a hard country, and you learn quickly if you're to survive. In an odd kind of way, you learn to love it, too.'

Only days earlier, Claire would have found this statement incomprehensible. Love this harsh, baking land with its rugged, inhospitable mountains, its flies, heat, dirt and squalor? Not in twenty years, she would have protested. But that was before she had held a thin, brown child on her lap, and watched the dogged endurance of men tilling the fields, women struggling desperately to raise families on a diet barely up to subsistence level.

At first, she had suspected that Ashley Wade was here because he was running away from something, or because he was a misfit from society. But now, having seen what it demanded of him not just to live here, but to function as a doctor, she was forced to modify her judgement. True, he was an individualist, maybe to the point of eccentricity. But in his rough, abrasive, often ill-tempered way, he cared about this place and its people, and that was the reason for his continued presence.

'Do you ever wonder what your mother would say if she could see you now?' she asked. 'Was this quite what she meant when she told you to get out of your mining village?'

'Probably not,' he conceded, 'but I think she would understand my reasons for being here, which is more than most women would be capable of doing.'

Claire stiffened.

'That's unfair, Ashley. All women aren't frivolous and self-seeking. And if you're including me in that generalisation, you're wrong. I *can* understand why you are here.'

'Ah, but you're not involved with me, Claire,' he said, with sour amusement. 'How would you feel if your what's-his-name...Jon...decided to chuck everything and incarcerate himself somewhere like this?'

'That's about as likely as my winning the Eurovision Song Contest!' she burst out with involuntary humour, the mere thought of Jon choosing to endure loneliness and discomfort causing her to bubble with laughter. But he did not join in, and she sobered, turning her head sideways so that her eyes could search his face in the shadows.

'Oh...I see! I'm sorry for being so thick,' she said. 'There was someone, wasn't there...and she wasn't mightily impressed by your decision to stay in Rio Negro? You're going to give me a ticking off now for being too inquisitive, I suppose.'

'No, I asked for it,' he replied evenly. 'And your diagnosis is spot on, Ms Mallory. There *was* someone. We were engaged.'

Claire listened to the silence for a moment or two, hearing her own pulse absurdly magnified by it.

'And now?' she ventured quietly.

'And now we aren't,' he supplied bluntly. She thought that was all the information he was going to impart, but after a while he continued, 'I met Lisa when I was Assistant Registrar at the hospital where she was a student nurse. She wasn't really too keen on my going into general practice at all. What she wanted was for me to make my way up the career ladder towards an eventual consultancy. Well, we weathered that one—just—but she turned down flat the prospect of coming here as my wife. I suppose I shouldn't blame her. It's a lot to ask. Love doesn't conquer all, you see.'

'I'm sorry,' Claire said. 'I see now why you took offence at what I said about shipping a nurse out from England.'

She cringed at the memory, but he merely shrugged.

'Your words touched a nerve,' he said. 'But you weren't to know. I'm not pining for Lisa, if that's what you think. I'm far too busy, damn it, and this place certainly puts one's personal problems in their true perspective. What she wanted wasn't really me, but a nice, tame husband with a nice, tame life all neatly mapped out for years ahead. However, it didn't work out, and there's no point in wasting time on regrets. It's a closed chapter—finished, done with. I rarely think about her.'

Claire found it hard to believe he could put behind him as finally as that the memory of a woman with whom he'd planned to spend the rest of his life.

'Just like that?' she asked. 'It can't be that easy. You must get incredibly lonely out here, sometimes.'

The moonlight revealed the whiteness of his teeth as a wicked grin enlivened his face.

'Is that a polite way of enquiring if I don't occasionally feel the need for a woman?' he asked bluntly, and Claire felt the prickling warmth of embarrassment reddening her face. She hoped it was not visible.

'No, it wasn't,' she denied hotly. 'I was thinking more about someone to talk to—someone who speaks your language, with whom you could discuss your problems, and be companionable. But of course, if that someone was also your wife...' She allowed that line of thought to peter out lamely, unwilling to take it any further.

'The answer is "yes" to both questions,' he said frankly. 'Although I'm probably one of nature's loners, there are times when I badly need someone to sound off to, or simply relax with. As for the other matter, I'm perfectly normal in that respect, Claire. It would be foolish to console myself with any of the local girls, because apart from the fact that they are all someone's wife, sister or daughter, every one of them is nominally my patient.'

'So no Yolandas?' Claire remarked carefully.

'Absolutely not. Not that I'm in any danger of being struck off, not out here, but... well, it's not ethical. It betrays the patient/doctor trust which I'm having a hard enough time building up. The water situation being what it is, cold showers aren't much of a remedy, either.'

He said this straight-faced, but with a grim edge of humour, and Claire looked up at him, startled by his earthy directness.

'Oh, Claire,' he said quietly. 'Don't you think I sometimes ache for the feel of a woman's body in my arms? The softness of her skin, and her hair——'

The unexpected vein of lyricism in this normally dour, practical man caught her off guard, and all the breath seemed to have been squeezed from her body, leaving her incapable of speech.

'Hair like moonlight,' he said, and lifting his hand, he loosed a strand of it from the confining ribbon at the nape of her neck, running his fingers through it. '"She walks in beauty, like the night...'"

Claire found her voice with difficulty.

'Oh, lord, not Byron, Ashley!' she protested, trying to lighten the sudden intensity of his mood with humour. 'I know it's been a long day, but...'

She gasped as he crushed her to him with one arm round her waist, the other hand tugging gently but insistently at her long hair, forcing her head back so that his mouth could claim hers, kissing her fiercely, but not roughly, easing her lips apart and invading them with his tongue. Claire's head swam. She had never felt like this when Jon kissed her, full of a sensuous excitement, as if she were embarking on a mysterious voyage to a place for which no maps existed. Like an explorer, eager to know what lay round the next bend in this new-found land...now his lips discovering the hollow of her throat, venturing along the line of her collarbone to her shoulder, now the crisp texture of his hair beneath her fingers. And then his hands finding their way upwards beneath her loose T-shirt, to close over her breasts.

The excitement mounted, and went on, and she made no attempt to prevent him, acquiescing gladly to the blissful torment which was sending her dizzy. It was he who let her go.

'Oh, my God, Claire!' he said abruptly. 'What am I doing?'

He took several paces away from her, running a hand distractedly through his hair, and then leaning against the fence. The deprivation, the frustration racking his body echoed her own, and, she realised, was probably far more urgent.

'Silly question!' he scoffed at himself. 'I knew very well what I was doing, but I shouldn't have been! It's a long time since I was alone with a girl in the moonlight, and you're damn desirable!'

Maybe it was because she had come so close to discovering the secret which had so far eluded her, had felt for the first time the powerful driving force of real passion and genuine desire, that Claire now felt cheated and let down. An unreasonable anger swept through her still quivering body.

'Please don't feel you have to apologise!' she exclaimed bitterly. 'It's hardly flattering!'

Her anger appeared to puzzle him.

'I don't mess with other men's women, as a rule, and I'll do you the courtesy of assuming you don't usually cheat on your bloke, either,' he said. 'Sometimes these things just happen. We were alone, you're in a strange environment, and as for me...'

'As you said, it's been a long time,' Claire said cynically. Was that all she had been, in those ecstatic moments? A woman's body... any woman? Or worse... 'I don't suppose you'd care to describe her to me, this Lisa of yours?'

The closeness, the rapport which had led them unawares into that brief eruption of passion, was fast evaporating. Her anger fuelled his, never slow to ignite.

'If you insist,' he said. 'She's blonde. Slim. About five foot six. Blue eyes, good body.'

He was describing her, item for item, and Claire forced down a sick rage.

'Great!' she said sarcastically. 'It's nice to know one's been used as a substitute.'

'At least I'm not betraying anyone's trust in me,' he retorted swiftly.

Claire bit her lip. She wasn't about to admit now that her involvement with Jon was all in the past.

'At least I kissed you, not a figment of my imagination,' she said scornfully, turning her back and stalking off without another word. It had been nothing more than a few moments of foolishness, but the trouble was, she still wished desperately that they had not ended as they had. The trouble was, she wanted him.

CHAPTER SEVEN

CLAIRE awoke in the pitch blackness of deepest night to a chaos of voices and sounds and movement. Someone was banging on the door and shouting loudly for the doctor, and from the urgency of it all she knew this had to be an emergency.

'*Sí—entiendo!* I hear you! I'm on my way!' she heard Ashley call out, and then the sound of the door being opened, a low, hurried conversation, and footsteps retreating. A very short while later she heard Ashley leave, presumably after having dressed quickly and grabbed his bag of essentials.

She lay for some time wondering just what had happened to require him in the middle of the night, and found herself worrying about people she scarcely knew, who were still no more than names or faces to her, and a cold thread of anxiety wound itself around her heart, nevertheless.

And then her thoughts turned to Ashley, coming home from whatever crisis had required his attention, already tired after a full, busy day, and an interrupted night. Coming home to a dark, silent house, as he had doubtless had to do many times since he came to live at San Stefano.

She struggled into her wrap and down the ladder into the living area, bumping into things in the gloom as she found the matches and lit the paraffin light hanging from the ceiling.

Getting the stove going was a trickier proposition, and Claire cursed as she tried to blow life into the coals, asking herself repeatedly why she was going to all this trouble for a man who had made her angry and humiliated only a few hours earlier.

Finally successful, she placed the coffee-pot on the hob, and stood waiting for the water to begin to bubble, wondering why she was making so much of a silly episode which was no more than the result of moonlight and proximity. Ashley, by his own admission, had lived a celibate life while in San Stefano. Was it any great surprise that, alone with a woman for the first time in who knew how long, he had succumbed to a perfectly natural inclination to make love? She should respect him for having held his passions in check, believing her to be already involved in a steady and committed relationship. Perhaps, in some odd way, Ashley Wade was a gentleman.

So far, so good. She went along with all of that. But what she could not forgive him was his confusing her with that girl he'd been engaged to marry, kissing her, Claire, touching her, while in his heart and mind *Lisa* was the one he held in his arms. She was insulted because he had not found her sufficiently attractive in her own right, only in so far as she resembled the girl he had once loved. And perhaps still loved, for all he denied it?

When he'd first told her about Lisa, she had been tempted to confess that her affair with Jon had been over before she left England. But not now. This had to be seen as an unguarded moment of physical attraction on both their parts, meaning nothing, and quickly forgotten. She did not want him to know that, not only was she free, but fiercely attracted to him, while to him she was no more than a surrogate.

She kept the coffee warm for perhaps another half-hour, before he returned, looking tired and grim, his face set in hard grooves of failure and regret. She knew the news would be bad, but a flicker of surprised gratitude lightened his features at the sight of her, and the aroma of brewing coffee.

'Claire? What are you doing up?'

'I heard you go out,' she whispered. 'I couldn't sleep. What was it?'

'Diego's youngest boy, Fernando. The child we saw today with measles,' he said shortly. 'He'd had a fit. By the time I got there, there was nothing to be done.'

Her eyes opened wide with incredulous horror.

'Nothing to be done?' she repeated. 'You mean he's...' She could not bring herself to say the word.

'Yes, Claire. He's dead. I told you that measles was a killer here.'

'No!' she cried, refusing to believe it, her eyes dark with shock and pain. The child she had held on her lap only that morning. She stared helplessly into his face, seeing depths of despair and futility which were new to her, and realising that she must control her grief, which must be as nothing compared to his.

'I'm worse than useless, really,' he said, flopping down on to the couch. 'Why don't I pack it in and push off? These people were without hope before I came, and there doesn't seem to be any I can offer them.'

Claire quickly filled a mug with coffee and took it over to him. Sitting beside him, she forced the beaker into his hands.

'Don't talk that way. Because there was nothing you could do tonight, it doesn't mean that you are useless,' she insisted. 'You're doing all that anyone could, and more. It isn't your fault you don't have sufficient support, financial or administrative. That's why we are here. And we *will* help you. I promise you.'

Her voice was steady and determined, and she knew that fulfilling that promise mattered more to her than anything she had ever done before. Here at last was a cause worthy of her energy, here was real need, which she, in her own small way, could do something to alleviate. Somewhere, in the past, she had lost the purpose which could have allowed her to help others, but here was a second chance, and she would not fail to carry it through.

He set the empty mug down on the floor, and took both her hands in a fierce grip. His eyes were a deep, intense blue, as despair was replaced by a different passion. A muscle jumped at the corner of his mouth, and beneath her wrap Claire's body began to tremble deliciously. Every nerve was alive and tingling, and close to the surface, her skin taut and stretched, so that the need to be touched was very nearly pain.

'You can help me *now*,' he said urgently. 'When I came in, I was so tired and drained, I could hardly see straight, but now I want to strip that robe from you, and make love to you until you scream for mercy. I need you, Claire. I need you very badly, right now!'

If it had really been her that he needed, Claire knew she would not have refused him the consolation she could have given him. Why should she, when it was no more than she wanted herself? But that was not so.

'You mean you want to make love to Lisa,' she said, her voice shaking. '*She's* the one you need. I'm sorry, Ashley, but I won't allow myself to be used in that way. And I'm not going to do anything tonight that I'll regret in the morning.'

He looked at her for a moment, his expression telling her nothing of what he was thinking.

'You're fortunate if that's all you'd have to regret in the morning,' he said quietly. 'Go on, then—take yourself off to bed, and out of harm's way. And don't wait up for me in future. OK?'

The next day, Greg felt much better, after a good night's rest, and it appeared he had escaped the more serious consequences of heat exhaustion. Basil, too, was exceptionally bright-eyed and bushy-tailed, eager to start shooting film again.

'I'm not denying I still fancy a drink like crazy,' he admitted to Claire. 'But that rotgut made me feel so lousy, there's no way I'm going to tangle with it any more, and since there's nothing else...' He shrugged. 'Seems Ashley can't afford to keep a bottle of Scotch in the house, and he manages OK without it.'

Claire murmured assent, privately thinking that a stiff Scotch might have defused some of last night's fierce tension.

'But will you stay on the wagon when you get home, Basil?' she queried.

His brow wrinkled in thought.

'I'm not making any promises, but I'll try. I mean, it's been a bit rough on my old lady, you know? Sometimes I wonder how she puts up with me.'

Claire had often wondered the same thing. Jane was a sweet girl, who worshipped Basil, but it could not have been easy for her. She was under no illusions that he would become a reformed character at the drop of a hat, but the mere fact that he had expressed an intention to try was a testimony to the change wrought in him by the brief sojourn in San Stefano... and to the influence of Ashley Wade, who, simply by being resolutely and unchangeably himself, had caused all of them to think more deeply about their own lives.

Claire felt this influence more profoundly than any of them, for in addition to the respect and admiration which he exacted from her, grudgingly at first, there was the disturbing effect he had on her as a woman. She knew now why she had so often been provoked and annoyed by his words and his manner. Her anger had been a refuge from her true feelings, and after last night it was no longer possible for her to ignore them. What she felt was not dislike, but desire, a sharp, fierce, reluctant need which she fought with every ounce of her strength, but still could not conquer.

She dared not give way to it. Her only attraction for him was her resemblance to Lisa, who had not loved him enough to share his chosen path. Last night, at the limit of his endurance, he had sought comfort in her body, and she had refused him. Perhaps he found that denial petty, set beside the life and death problems he faced, but Claire could not give herself causally and take brief affairs in her stride. If she had given him that impression, it was mistakenly, and she did not know how to correct it without appearing cold and uncaring.

But he had nothing to say to her about what had happened...or not happened...between them the night before. Neither his eyes nor his words made any reference to it, and Claire understood that, for him, the matter was closed. He would not allude to it again.

In any event, he had other priorities. Two more children in the village had measles, and although neither was seriously affected, Ashley was worried about the possibility of an epidemic. She was beginning to appreciate the fraught, difficult, agonising business of being a single-handed doctor in a remote, poverty-stricken area where he was still seen as something of an intruder, but wondered if something in his nature enabled him to switch off his personal life so easily. Was that what Lisa had resented? It would take a rare breed of woman to live here, enduring all the hardship and difficulties, as well as being a poor second in her man's life, Claire thought, watching him covertly as he discussed with Greg the necessity of implementing a programme of vaccination.

Greg turned to Claire, interrupting her thoughts.

'If the company did agree to sponsor such a programme, do you think Harold would consider sending you out to do a follow-up article?'

The suggestion caught her off guard. It was logical enough, and if Harold was pleased with what she turned in after this trip, then she was the obvious person for the job. But that would once again throw her into close contact with Ashley Wade, and Claire was not at all sure that she wanted this.

Not because she found him rude, provocative, eccentric and infuriating, even though he was all of those things at times—and sometimes all four of them together! The question now was—could she take that measure of involvement with him? Wouldn't it be wiser to go home knowing that she would not see him again, rather than prolong this dangerous and pointless attraction?

It alarmed her to think that she had become so unprofessional as to consider turning down a job because a man's touch set her all of a dither, the look in his eyes made her want to fall headlong into his arms. Was she falling in love? she asked herself incredulously.

As always, when she was not immediately ready with a swift answer, Ashley jumped to the wrong conclusion.

'I think Claire would like to say that she's had enough of Rio Negro, and wild horses wouldn't drag her back here again,' he said sardonically. 'Go ahead, Claire. You don't need hesitate to spare my sensibilities. I'd sooner have someone whose heart was in the job.'

It was a dangerous indicator of her own emotions that, instead of being merely indignant, she was hurt by his words.

'Don't presume to know where my heart is, just because I don't wear it on my sleeve!' she retorted. 'I've been shocked and appalled by a great deal that I've seen here, but I don't hold it against San Stefano, or its people. It's not their fault. I'd be perfectly willing to do a follow-up, but I prefer to work with people who aren't antagonistic towards me, so it might be better all round if another journalist did the job!'

Ashley had promised to take Claire and the others with him on one of his sporadic treks into the mountains to the more remote settlements, but he was reluctant to leave the village for a day or two, as he was watching to see if there were an appreciable increase in the number of measles cases.

Claire spent those days working on her article, roughing out a preliminary draft from her notes, and when she had got as far as she could she asked Ashley to read it through to ascertain that he agreed with her facts.

He read in total silence, a brooding expression on his faces, and she began to feel anxious, an emotion that was foreign to her, since she was methodical and careful in her preparation, and by the time she had got to this stage she had checked and double-checked. This, she supposed ruefully, was the result of being emotionally involved with the man she was writing about, and an overwhelming relief swept over her as he looked up at last, with a brief smile.

'I can't fault that on anything,' he said. 'I honestly hadn't realised how much you were taking in while you were following me round with your notepad. And I like the way you write about Rio Negro, condemning what's wrong without being strident and hysterical. It's a measured, factual, very moving piece of work. Well done, Claire. I admit you drive me clean up the wall sometimes, but there's no denying you're a damn good journalist.'

She could not prevent herself from colouring with pleasure at this ungrudging praise.

'You send me bananas, too, but we'll have to accept one another for what we're worth, and forget...or set aside our differences,' she conceded. 'When do you think we'll be able to set out on our trek?'

'Hopefully, tomorrow. I'm going down to the village now, to check the measles situation.'

She jumped up eagerly. 'Can I come along?'

'If you wish.' He shrugged. 'But I can't promise you any new material.'

It wasn't the hope of new material that drew her to the poor houses of San Stefano, but the children, who touched a chord in her that she had not known existed, because she had never before been in close contact with such little ones. She hated the idea of them dying of what, in England, was considered a mild, if troublesome childhood ailment.

'I can see it wasn't the pleasure of my company that attracted you,' Ashley said, a strange note creeping into his voice, watching with some surprise as she picked them up, played with them, enjoying the little hands tugging at the blonde hair which was such a novelty in their world. 'They seem to like you, too. You should marry your fellow and have half a dozen of your own.'

Claire smiled gently.

'I don't think Jon is exactly first-class father material,' she said lightly.

He looked into her eyes, his own suddenly full of penetrating and urgent intensity.

'Then for God's sake unload him, and find yourself someone who *is*,' he said forcefully.

It seemed as unlikely a dream as flying to the moon, and as she returned his fierce gaze it came to her with a force that was almost violent, and blindingly obvious, that bearing a child was the natural sequel to the way she had felt when Ashley held her in his arms. That driving urge to belong to a man, to touch and possess, was created for that purpose. They were one and the same. She wanted to be his, and bring his child into the world. It that were not love, then Claire didn't know what was. It followed automatically that she must love him.

A man she had known only days, who was ruthlessly dedicated to his work, who had given up the woman he loved in order to live here and fight the unequal battle against sickness and poverty? A man to whom she was no more than a good journalistic brain, a female body, and a passing likeness to his ex-fiancée? It was ludicrous. It was impossible. It had happened.

'Find someone who is? Just like that?' she demanded angrily. 'Should I get a questionnaire, do you think? "Are you a good father?" "Can you support a large family?" That sort of thing? It doesn't work that way, Ashley, as you should know. You didn't pick Lisa with the aid of a computer, did you?'

He stared at her, surprised by her agitation, his eyes probing deep beneath the surface, and Claire looked down at the baked earth, anxious he should not discover the truth.

'No, the computer would have done a better job,' he admitted wryly. 'I'll try to keep out of your private life. Certainly, I'm ill qualified to dish out advice.'

Claire said little as she accompanied him on the rest of his visits. She had foolishly fallen in love with him, but there was little to be gained by letting him discover this. It could only embarrass him and make her appear ridiculous.

'There don't appear to be any more cases of measles,' he said, as they walked back through the swift, tropical sunset, which crimsoned the sky behind the mountains in a flood of wild, roseate beauty. 'I really must make that trip into the hills. There's a girl expecting a baby whom I'm rather anxious about. She's young and scared, her husband badly wants a son, and she's had two miscarriages already. Are you sure you're all up to the trip?'

'I *want* to come,' Claire insisted. 'So will Greg and Basil, I'm sure. I don't see any of us chickening out at this stage.'

'No,' he agreed, surprisingly. 'You'll stay the course, I reckon, although a week ago I wouldn't have bet my shirt on it.'

And if she couldn't have his love, Claire reckoned she would have to be satisfied that she had at least earned a measure of his respect.

Midway between the last straggling dwellings of San Stefano and Ashley's house, the swish of a red skirt caused her to catch a glimpse of two figures, half-hidden by a stunted clump of trees. A girl and a young man standing close together, she with her hands on her hips, looking up at him provocatively, hand flung back.

'That's Yolanda, Pilar's daughter,' Claire said, peering into the swiftly gathering dusk.

Ashley nudged her arm. 'It's rude to stare at courting couples, Claire. Give them a bit of privacy, and stop gawping, as we say in Yorkshire,' he grinned.

'What a lovely word!' she chuckled, and then a frown creased her forehead. 'But, Ashley...that young man with Yolanda ... I'm sure it's one of those two who were staring at me, back in Aguas Calientes. Remember ... the first night we met?'

'As if I could forget! I thought they'd sent me a cover girl from *Vogue*, who was scared of mules,' he teased, slowing his walk and following her gaze. But it was almost dark now, and the couple were no more than a blur among the trees. 'What makes you think it's the same man?'

For some reason she did not understand, a prickle of foreboding crept along Claire's spine as she recalled that night, and the unpleasantly careful scrutiny.

'I know it is. I recognised him,' she insisted. 'And anyhow, who is there in San Stefano who wears good American jeans like those—apart from Greg?'

'So Yolanda has a boyfriend from the city, who is probably far too sophisticated for her,' he mused, frowning. 'She's probably trying to persuade him to take her back there, away from all this. I'll have a word with her, next time Pilar sends her up to my place. Young girls are often seduced away into towns, believing they'll find a better life there. What they do find, more often, is greater poverty than they left behind, and a life of degradation and crime.'

'From what I recall of Yolanda, she may not take too much notice of a lecture,' Claire said. 'You'd be better advised warning her mother.'

He sighed. 'It's not that simple, Claire. Pilar has so many other children, and problems of her own. She might be glad for Yolanda to move out and make one less, so to speak. In a way, they all half believe this Dick Whittington myth about the cities, although they know very well what they see there. But I'll do what I can, when we get back from our trip.'

Claire puzzled a little longer about the coincidental appearance in San Stefano of a man who had been watching her in Aguas Calientes, and then dismissed it from her mind as insignificant. There were too many other things to think about, and preparations to be made before they all turned in for an earlier night than usual.

In the morning, they were all astir before it was fully light. After a makeshift breakfast of bread and coffee, they saddled up the mules and loaded the baggage, working quickly and quietly. They were all more experienced now than the clumsy novices who had set out from Aguas Calientes.

Claire's spirits lifted with a sensation of freedom and excitement as they rode out into the glimmering daybreak. It was a relief to get out of the house, which had, for the last few days, seemed to shut her in with her own emotions, from which there was no escape.

She took them along as baggage, of course; it had already been decided that they would leave San Stefano on their return. They had amassed all the information they required, seen at first-hand a good cross-section of the work Ashley was doing, and the time had come to get on with the next stage of their job. Greg had business commitments he must keep, and Claire and Basil had deadlines to meet, to fit in with publishing schedules.

So she had no more than a few more days to spend with Ashley, days she could probably count on the fingers of one hand. And then he would be someone she had once met, in the past, and might not meet again, a memory which would haunt and torment her in the months and years to come. Would it grow more distant, more endurable with time? Claire prayed that it would...and yet some part of her did not want to forget. She needed to hold on to the love she had unexpectedly found, however painful that would prove.

She forced these sombre thoughts from her mind. She had these last days, which no one could take from her, and she was determined to experience them to the utmost, so that every detail of the way he looked, spoke acted, remained clear in her mind. It would have to last her a long time.

The lonely, rugged mountains, which had frightened her a little when they first rode into them so short a time ago, exhilarated her now. She relished the freedom of the open sky and the empty land all around. Ironically, now it was almost time to leave, she had come to terms with Rio Negro, as if loving Ashley had taught her to look at it through his eyes, understanding the bonds which kept him here.

Nor was the land as empty as it at first appeared. Along the trail, they passed isolated hamlets and farmsteads, and at every one there was someone who wanted to see the doctor. They camped at night in a field behind one of those lonely farms, and it was late before the children of the family could be persuaded to stop hanging around these interesting visitors and go to bed. It wasn't every day that a lady with long, silvery hair, and a man with cameras, paid them so much attention!

Basil had spent much of the day snapping and clicking. He already had more than enough pictures for the *World Focus* article, but the scenery and people inspired him to take more, for a book of his own work he was compiling for future publication. When he crawled into the tent he shared with Greg, he was exhausted, satisfied... and, of course, sober, a state to which he was becoming more accustomed as the days passed.

'I just hope he'll be able to keep it up when we get back to the everyday world, full of temptations such as bars, hotels and parties,' Claire reflected quietly.

She and Ashley were sitting along by the camp fire he had made, a little way from where the tents were pitched, drinking strong black coffee, while the mules grazed contentedly nearby.

'Since he has to live in that world, it's a chance we have to take,' he replied. 'But there is help available, if he'll only accept it.'

'Mm. I think I'll have a quiet word with Jane, his girlfriend, when I get back to England,' Claire decided. 'She'll be delighted by the change in him, and I know she'll want to give him all the encouragement she can.'

He glanced obliquely at her, a faint smile touching his mouth.

'And you were the one who said we weren't responsible for one another's foibles, and should mind our own business,' he reminded her. 'You didn't really mean it, did you? Perhaps you should have been a doctor. You'd have made quite a good one, I can tell from the way you've helped me.'

Claire licked her lips. She still felt haunted by a deeply buried sense of failure, and did not want to be drawn into a discussion which might rake up the past.

'Any reasonably intelligent person could do what I did ... perhaps more, with a little instruction,' she said carefully. 'I think, with the best will in the world, you're going about things the wrong way.'

'Ah. Ms Mallory is about to pronounce judgement,' he said drily. 'I suppose I must sit at your feet and listen while you tell me how to run my life and work.'

'Don't be flippant, Ashley. I'm serious,' she said impatiently. 'You're one man, and you're trying to do far too much. You can't go on indefinitely patrolling this huge area, seeing and treating every patient individually. So far you've managed to survive, but eventually it will ruin your health, or kill you, and where will all these people be then?'

'I'm asking myself whether your concern is for the patients or the physician,' he said, looking at her so intently that Claire dropped her gaze.

'Both, of course,' she said briskly. 'My father once said a lot of sickness will cure itself, using the body's own defences.'

'He probably added, given cleanliness, good food, and fresh water, which he could take for granted, and I can't,' Ashley interrupted caustically.

'Agreed, but why not re-think your role? Become less of a single-handed curer of all ills, and more of an educator. Delegate. In every small village or settlement, train someone to deal with basic problems, and to know when to refer them to you. Teach people more about hygiene and correct nutrition, nag them to build latrines, fence off their drinking water from animals, grow more leafy veg and soya beans—that sort of thing.' She laughed nervously. 'An ounce of prevention is worth more than several pounds of cure. Another of my father's maxims.'

'It sounds as if your father and my mother would have done well to get together,' he said. He was silent for a while, and she thought he was angry, but then she realised he was merely thoughtful. 'I think I'd better sleep on all that advice.'

He spread out his sleeping-bag on the ground, equidistant between the tents and the dying fire. Claire rose to go. She had risked an almighty put-down by presuming to advise him, and there was no point in antagonising him by pursuing it further.

'Goodnight,' she said quietly.

He caught her arm as she made to pass him, holding it lightly, so that she could have shaken it off easily had she wanted to.

'You look so beautiful, Claire, with your hair loose like that,' he said, a catch making his voice ragged. 'If I weaken during the night, and come crawling into your tent, will you turn me out?'

So beautiful? So much like Lisa, she thought bitterly, and promptly removed his hand. She wasn't going to play second fiddle to memory, however much she loved him.

'You can count on it, Ashley,' she said steadily, and turned her back on him. But he would never know how much effort it had cost her to make her refusal clear.

CHAPTER EIGHT

SOME sort of bush telegraph had obviously been at work, for before they could saddle up and set off in the morning a number of people had trudged, or in some cases had been stretcher-carried, a considerable distance to see Ashley, including a badly scared teenage boy who had been bitten by a snake.

A crude application of leaves covered the wound, and Ashley gave a wry smile.

'Another of these home cures which are so prevalent,' he told Claire. 'This one won't actually do any harm, but neither will it cure the bite. Some of these miraculous claims people make for such remedies probably work because in that particular instance, the snake involved was not poisonous. But one should not underestimate the power of belief. Shock and fright are universal reactions to being bitten, and the fact that our young friend here believed the leaves would do some good probably helped to slow down his pulse-rate and prevent the poison spreading.'

'So this snake was poisonous?' Claire said, alarmed. 'How can you tell?'

'Because it's left two definite fang marks in the skin, whereas a non-poisonous snake would have left only two rows of teeth marks. I'm going to give him an anti-venom injection. There's nothing to suggest he might suffer an allergic shock reaction, but watch him for me while I attend to the others, just in case.'

'Excuse me!' Claire said, watching him give the injection. 'What exactly am I looking out for? We don't see much snakebite in Sussex, and I don't know what allergic shock looks like.'

'Point taken,' he grinned. 'Cool, damp skin with a cold sweat, weak pulse, any trouble breathing—and of course, loss of consciousness.'

Claire sat dutifully by the boy, chatting desultorily in her fractured Spanish, surprising herself by how much she could express, even if it were ungrammatical, which she could not have done a fortnight ago. She was relieved to note that he suffered no ill effects, and soon it was time for them to leave this tiny outpost of civilisation.

Once again, her world was the mountains, the now familiar swaying of the mule beneath her, and Ashley's erect back ahead. The sun was already hot, but she had begun to accept its intense, burning brightness, adapting herself to it rather than fighting against it. She tugged down the brim of her hat to cover the nape of her neck, and grinned ruefully as she looked down at the sun-tanned backs of her hands. She'd be a rave at parties, with skin like old shoe-leather!

Parties. London. Buses and taxis, crowds jostling along the pavements, queues in shops . . . it all seemed so far away and unreal, and with a start she realised that she wouldn't care if she never went home, but stayed here, helping Ashley support the heavy load of his work, giving him whatever he needed to make his life easier. She had to remind herself sternly that he did not really need *her*—she represented only an extra pair of hands and the ephemeral comfort of a woman's body. She couldn't settle for that.

As they ate their lunch of bread and goat's cheese, Ashley told them a little about the expectant mother they were going to see.

'Maria-Elena is young, not more than eighteen, but already she has had two miscarriages and a still birth,' he said. 'She is Tomas's second wife—his first died childless, and he's almost beside himself with anxiety to produce a son. I tried talking him into letting Maria-Elena stay with her sister in San Stefano until after the birth. That way I could be sure of being there for the confinement. But he won't let her go. He's much older than she, and fiercely possessive. I'm afraid for the effect on her health...possibly her life...of further pregnancies. If this child is born alive, and male, I'm going to suggest strongly that she takes steps to avoid having any more.'

'What if it's alive and healthy, but a girl?' Claire demanded swiftly.

'If that's the case, I might as well save my breath,' he said. 'My opinion won't fight centuries of custom, Claire. Tomas sees a son as his right. Maria-Elena will see it that way, too.'

She was silent for a while as she mounted her mule, but her desire to know how much headway the views she had expressed the previous night had made was too strong to be suppressed.

'Do I take it you've given some thought to our conversation yesterday?' she ventured cautiously.

'Don't I always?' he grinned evasively.

'No. You're stubborn and pig-headed,' she retorted. 'I don't know why I bother.'

'I don't know either, Claire,' he said, the blue eyes blazing into hers, and the directness of his gaze threw her into a sweet confusion she fought hard to conceal beneath a fragile veneer of calm. 'But yes, stubborn and pig-headed as I am, I *have* thought about what you said, and I do concede that there is some sense in it. That's as far as I'm going to go for the moment, so don't try pushing me further.'

'I suppose that means that the minute I'm no longer around, you'll simply carry on as you've been accustomed to doing, and one day I'll be reading a few brief lines about you in the obituary column of *The Times*,' she said, with terse anger.

'Will it worry you?' he asked lightly.

She gave a snort of annoyance. 'Heaven knows why it should! But I prefer to think of you saddling up Modesta, or grumbling at Pilar's cooking...if I think of you at all,' she added grudgingly, hoping that her denial of any deeper involvement was convincing.

They continued to ride, climbing higher into the mountains and dropping down again into a lonely green valley.

'Not too far, now,' Ashley said, as the narrow trail widened into a dirt track which was obviously well used. 'Tomas and a few others actually chose this valley because the land here is fairly fertile, and has possibilities. They're pioneers, in a sense. But they're finding it a struggle because of the remoteness and inaccessibility.'

'I certainly wouldn't like to be having a baby here, so far from any kind of medical help.' Claire shuddered. 'What on earth will Maria-Elena do if there are complications?'

'That's precisely what worries me,' Ashley frowned. 'There's a local woman who fancies herself as a midwife, but she couldn't deal with anything which deviated too far from a normal birth. And she's full of strange superstitions.'

Even as they considered his words, a shout alerted them, and they saw a young man racing down the track towards them. He was panting heavily and out of breath by the time he reached them, and his words came out in gasps as he collapsed against Ashley's mule.

There was obviously some kind of emergency, and Claire, who had picked up more Spanish than the others, knit her brows as she listened.

'It's Maria-Elena—I think she's started in labour,' she said. 'Somehow, word must have reached them that we were on our way.'

'That's right,' Ashley agreed tersely. 'This is Juan, Tomas's brother, who lives with them. The baby is almost a month early, and with Maria-Elena's history . . . well, let's not waste time talking.'

He kneed his mule onwards and the others followed, leaving Juan to recover his breath before catching up with them.

Claire had time to notice that Tomas's farm, as Ashley had indicated, showed signs of being more prosperous than many of those in the immediate neighbourhood of San Stefano. But the family paid a price for their adventurousness, being so far away from even that rudimentary civilisation.

Tomas came running out to meet them, a small, harrassed-looking man, perhaps in his late thirties, wringing his hands and giving thanks to God that the doctor was here, just when he was needed.

'God moves in a mysterious way, so it's said, but it certainly is one mighty coincidence that Maria-Elena should go into premature labour on this very day,' Ashley muttered to Claire as they all dismounted from their mules.

Basil and Greg looked nervously at one another.

'Oh, man!' the photographer exclaimed. 'I mean— include me out on this one, will you?'

'Absolutely!' Greg agreed with feeling. 'We'd only get in the way.'

Ashley smiled.

'I should stay well out of it, if I were you. Tomas will show you where to graze the mules. Do me a favour, and keep him out of my way, if possible. He's too anxious and agitated to be of any help.'

He turned to Claire with a swift, appraising look in his eyes. 'Stick around. I might need *you*.'

The blood drained from her face, and her legs felt weak, about to collapse beneath her. This was not unrolling bandages in the controlled conditions of the surgery, or holding a child's hand while Ashley gave it an injection. This was an emergency in the making. A young woman who had previously suffered miscarriages was about to give premature birth, and she, who had never witnessed a normal confinement in the hygienic safety of a hospital, was expected to help.

'Oh, no!' she said weakly. 'Oh, no, Ashley, I can't...don't ask me!'

He looked at her taut, bloodless face for a moment, and then spoke sharply, without pity.

'Claire, I'm going to need another pair of hands for this one. The midwife-woman is apparently away somewhere, delivering another baby, leaving Tomas, who would be useless, Juan, who's too young, and their old mother, who's bedridden. So pull yourself together, and let's get on with the job!'

He addressed her impersonally, as if she were no more than the most junior of student nurses, who had briefly lost her nerve, and needed a swift jerk of authority to remind her of her duty. This detached, ruthless attitude would have set Claire seething with resentment only a few days ago, but now it brought her abruptly to her senses.

Ashley needed help, and there was no one else but herself who could supply it. A girl was having a baby—

two lives were possibly at risk, while she stood dithering with fright and indecision, her mind racing back across the years to the night of the train crash, the blood, the fear and the panic. She'd turned away then, not only from the accident, but from a life which would have involved her with the suffering of others. But she had been young and unprepared, and there had been others present with the skills and abilities to help.

Now there was not. She was at a remote farm in the mountains of Central America, with the man she loved, who was prepared to give his whole life to this cause, and here she was, hesitating again at crisis point.

'All right,' she whispered nervously, clenching her hands and searching desperately for a courage she feared she did not possess. 'I'll help—for what it's worth.'

His smile warmed her briefly.

'Don't worry. Just do what I tell you,' he said in a calm, reassuring voice. 'This may turn out to be quite straightforward, after all.'

Inside the house the young mother-to-be was walking up and down, clutching at her distended stomach and occasionally muttering what might have been either a prayer or an expletive as the pain gripped her. But her eyes shone with hope as she saw Ashley, and she welcomed him with a brave determination.

Claire knew an instinctive sympathy and liking for this girl, still struggling to give her husband a son after three disappointments. There was an unmistakable intelligence about her, and her courage was not in doubt. The only other occupant of the room was an old woman lying on a bed in the corner, whose eyes had the glazed expression of senility, and who clearly would have been no help at all.

Ashley took a list from his bag and gave it to Claire.

'Here's a list of the things I told Maria-Elena to have ready from her seventh month onwards. Look them out for me. And see that the fire is burning in the kitchen, and that there's plenty of hot water.'

Claire took several deep breaths to get her own nerves under control. Nothing very dire was actually happening yet, and might not for some time. Maria-Elena was still actively pacing the room and, now that the doctor had so fortuitously arrived, seemed remarkably confident and self-possessed.

She was the one having the baby. Ashley was the one who would have to deliver it. I'm only the dogsbody, she told herself, so why should I be scared? This brisk dose of self-ridicule did not entirely banish her apprehension, but it helped and she applied herself to doing as she was bidden, checking off the items as she found them: a box of very clean cloths, a bar of soap, a clean nailbrush ... Oh, and she mustn't forget the water ...

Ashley persuaded Maria-Elena to lie down while he examined her, reassuring himself and her that everything was going as it should, even though, yes, the baby was a little early. As soon as he had finished his examination, she resumed pacing up and down, and Claire spread clean sheets on the bed, as directed.

'Shouldn't she be lying down?' she asked anxiously. Every film she had ever seen, or book she had read, had the mother prone and immobilised, with white-coated attendants flitting around like acolytes before a shrine.

'There's no reason why she should, yet, if she's happier as she is,' he assured her. 'There's a lot to be said in favour of home confinements, as opposed to the hospital style, where the woman is more or less imprisoned—wired, tubed and completely helpless.'

Claire was never sure, afterwards, how long they spent like this, with Maria-Elena pacing the room, but it seemed to go on indefinitely. Ashley had all his equipment in readiness, clean and sterile, and from time to time he listened to the foetal heartbeat, strong and regular, occasionally sending Claire to tell the impatient Tomas that all was well, and proceeding normally.

When the contractions began to come faster, and the waters broke, Maria-Elena was finally persuaded to lie on the bed. She smiled confidingly up at Claire, and as her eyes met the large, dark ones a strange thing happened. Claire found her own fear began to recede in the face of the other girl's trust. She was totally involved, and no longer afraid.

The pains grew stronger, and they encouraged her to take deep, slow, regular breaths, but Maria-Elena seemed to have no need of the sophisticated analgesics that women of the developed world demanded and took for granted during labour. The pain was expected, recognised for what it was, and coped with.

The birth proceeded quickly now, with Ashley encouraging Maria-Elena to bear down during the contractions, and equally importantly, to resist doing so between them, so as not to cause tearing which would later require stitches. Claire's qualms had vanished long ago, in the excitement of watching the baby's head gradually appear with each push, and she mopped, cleaned, encouraged, and gripped the other woman's hand, perspiration beading her own face as if it were she who was working hard to bring this baby into the world.

At last the face appeared, and Ashley took it in his hands, allowing first one shoulder to emerge and then the other. A final, triumphant push from Maria-Elena, and the infant slipped out into his waiting hands.

Claire could hardly restrain her shout of joy and relief. '*Niño*, Maria-Elena!' she cried. '*Tu hijo!* Your son!'

Quickly and deftly, Ashley cleaned the mucus form the baby's nose and mouth, and allowed himself a relieved sigh as it began to breathe. He tied and cut the cord, cleaned the child with a warm, damp cloth, and with the minimum of delay handed him to his mother, who was waiting eagerly, eyes shining, all the pain quickly forgotten.

Ashley's eyes met Claire's across the bed, over the head of the young woman now blissfully absorbed in the newborn son at her breast.

'Not so bad, was it?' he asked laconically.

'It was tremendous!' she responded instinctively, buoyed up by the wholly creative tension and exhilaration of this marvellous process she had somehow managed to assist. 'I'd no idea it could be so...so satisfying!'

'You're still shaking,' he smiled. 'That's a perfectly natural reaction, believe me. You were great—thanks for your help. But you aren't having all the pleasure or all the kudos. *I* get to tell Tomas that he finally has his son and heir! You keep an eye on Maria-Elena while I go and impart the glad tidings.'

Claire collapsed willingly on to a stool, and sat hugging herself as she watched Maria-Elena peacefully nursing the baby. Today she had laid a ghost that had haunted her for many years, and suddenly she felt exhausted and light-headed at the same time, as if its exorcism had both relieved her of a burden and drained her of an emotion she had carried as mental excess baggage for far too long.

Since she came to Rio Negro, she had learned to look pain, suffering and hardship in the face, knowing she was doing something to help relieve it, and just now she had coped with the potential trauma and danger of birth. Had she finally put behind her the scared girl who had run like a rabbit at the sight of blood?

Blood!

Claire's senses were suddenly alert as she glanced at the woman on the bed. A little bleeding was normal, and to be expected, Ashley had said, but surely, not so much as this...

Claire did not panic. Quietly, without alarming Maria-Elena, she went to the door, surprised to find that it was still daylight, and what had seemed so long a time to her could have been no more than a few hours. Over by the paddock, she could see the men, Tomas wringing Ashley's hand fiercely, Basil and Greg slapping the father on the back.

Strange how fathers always got the congratulations, having done so little of the hard work, she thought wryly. But she did not lose time pondering on the possible injustice of that. Quickly she walked across the stretch of stubbly grass, and tapped Ashley on the arm.

'Can you come for a minute—at once?' she said, trying to convey urgency without panic. He must have grasped her intention, for he forestalled Tomas, telling him his wife and son were not quite ready to see him yet, and followed her back to the house.

'What's the problem?'

'Maria-Elena. I could be wrong, but it looks to me as if she's losing too much blood.'

'No, you're not wrong,' he said shortly, as soon as he closed the door behind them. Claire watched anxiously as he massaged the girl's stomach and womb, but despite his efforts the blood continued to flow faster than ever, and a horrible cold fear gripped Claire as she stood by, helpless.

This can't happen, she thought frantically. They had brought a live, healthy child into the world, but the brave girl who had persevered in the face of failure to bear a son now looked in danger of bleeding to death.

Ashley's face looked grim, and for the first time, Claire saw fear in Maria-Elena's dark eyes as the blood drained from her. She reached for Claire's hand and grasped it tightly, holding on with desperation, and Claire gripped it hard in return, wishing wretchedly that there were more she could do to help.

Ashley acted swiftly. She saw him reach for his medical bag, and quickly insert an ampoule into a syringe. She saw him giving Maria-Elena the injection. And then there was a buzzing in her ears, and a strange sensation of everything being blurred around the edges. From a long way distant, she heard Ashley's voice, cool and measured, cutting through the fuzziness of her muddled senses.

'Claire,' he said, calmly and distinctly, 'I'm sorry, but I can't cope with two patients. So take yourself outside, if you must, but kindly don't faint here!'

She came round, sitting on the grass outside the farmhouse, leaning up against the wall, surrounded by the darkness of the swiftly gathering night.

'Oh, what an idiot I am!' she breathed disgustedly, when she could finally speak.

'Not at all!' Greg said stoutly. 'You performed wonders, helping Ashley deliver the baby.'

'Man, I'd have fainted at the first hint of pain,' Basil backed him up. 'If my Jane ever decides she wants kids, I won't be one of the brave fathers in the delivery-room.'

Claire smiled weakly, grateful for their praise, but it was misplaced, she reflected soberly. When it came to the point, she had proved a broken reed.

'How's Maria-Elena?' she demanded, looking from one anxious face to another, and realising that no one knew any more than she did. Tomas was hopping from one foot to the other, chain-smoking foul-smelling cheroots, but the house door remained resolutely closed on doctor and patient.

They waited in silence and growing apprehension until at last Ashley emerged, looking very tired. He grasped Tomas's arm briefly before letting him go inside, and turned to the anxious little knot of watchers with a drawn smile.

'She'll be OK,' he said.

Claire exhaled heavily. She wanted to share her relief with the others, but her shame at her own behaviour was so great that she could not look Ashley directly in the face. Excusing herself with a swift gesture of her hand, she got up and stumbled round the other side of the house, where she leaned against the wall, eyes closed, taking deep breaths of the night air.

She knew the steady hands on her shoulders were Ashley's, and her eyes flew open, guiltily searching his face in the shadows.

'I'm all right. Just leave me alone,' she begged. 'Maria-Elena will make it—that's what matters.'

'Of course she will. She'll need to take it easy for a while, and I don't think she should risk another pregnancy, but Tomas is so delighted with his son, right now he's ready to listen to anything I suggest. So no problems there. It's you I'm worried about at the moment.'

'Me?' she shrugged. 'Don't. I'm not worth it. I failed you when you most needed me. I could have told you I'd be useless in a situation like that.'

'Don't talk nonsense.' He gave her a slight shake. 'You did sterling work, all the while the baby was being born, and you'd never seen a birth before, with or without complications. Anyone would have been a little overcome.' He studied her intently. 'What makes you say you expected to be useless?'

Claire gave a long, weary sigh. She was too tired and emotionally strained to hang on to her guilty secret any longer, and perhaps only by telling someone would she finally come to terms with it. She was afraid of Ashley's contempt, but right now, it seemed that not to tell him would be to live a lie. She might never see him again after her return to England, but she owed it to him and to herself to reveal the real Claire, with all her faults and inadequacies, instead of hiding behind a cool façade put up to conceal whom she really was.

'When I was young, I very much wanted to follow my father's example, and become a doctor. You were right about that,' she told him. 'But one day, I witnessed a horrific accident—a train crash—and instead of staying to see if I could help, I panicked and bolted. I just couldn't take it, and I knew then that I didn't have the guts for such a hard profession.' She took a deep breath. 'So now you know, Dr Wade.'

She looked up again, steeling herself to meet the scorn and disgust she expected to find in his eyes. But his expression scarcely altered.

'Did you never tell your father why you had changed your mind?' he asked. 'Knowing you, I expect you kept it to yourself.'

'I couldn't bring myself to tell him,' she said miserably. 'I was so ashamed. I know he never really understood my decision.'

'Not surprising—most of us aren't mind-readers, Claire,' he said soberly. 'How old were you when this happened?'

She frowned. 'Fifteen. Why?'

He tightened his hands on her shoulders, but instead of shaking her, drew her closer so that her head rested against him.

'Oh...Claire...you little fool,' he said softly. 'You changed your whole life on account of the entirely understandable fear of a girl little more than a child? Don't you know most doctors have reactions of panic like that when they are young and untried? The first time in theatre...the first time we deliver a baby...I was scared as hell, twenty-four hours a day, during my first stint in Casualty. But we recover and get over it. We press on. Your father could have told you that, had you only confided in him. Instead, you buttoned it all up inside, and you've been carrying around this quite unnecessary load of guilt ever since.'

He took her chin in his hand and tilted it upwards, looking down sternly into her eyes.

'I've seen the way you've coped since you came to San Stefano, how you've helped me, how you've faced problems and diseases you would never see at home, and I admit, I didn't make it easy for you. I was mistaken enough to think you were a spoiled socialite! Now I know how much fear you had to overcome, it makes what you've done all the more praiseworthy. Claire, you've more guts than any woman I've met, so all this blaming yourself and feeling inadequate had got to stop, right now. Do you hear me?'

The sentiments he expressed filled her with a flooding warmth, but they were delivered in such a firm, hard manner that Claire could not resist a little smile, even though, to her horror, tears of long-pent-up emotion and relief were running down her cheeks.

'Yes, Doctor,' she said meekly. 'Whatever you say.'

His face was very close to hers, and she saw his mouth twist wryly. The need to be kissed by him was too strong to deny—and she *had* to feel his mouth on hers again. The intensity of this compulsion shocked her, but she could not help it. Her eyes were full of naked invitation as she looked up at him through her tears.

'It's been said that a woman can't look beautiful while she's crying,' he said raggedly. 'I know that's not true.'

'If I'm so desirable, why don't you kiss me?' she heard herself whisper, knowing that if he did, it would not stop there, while they were both being swept forwards on a wave of unbearable tension.

For a moment, he hesitated, and it was as if some unseen magnetism was drawing them inexorably towards one another. And then he disengaged her, almost roughly.

'I'm not some damn prescription you can take to make you feel better!' he rasped.

'No?' she countered, stung by the harshness of this rejection. 'But that's what you expected me to be, the night Diego's boy died. It's all one-sided with you, Ashley, isn't it?'

He fished a handkerchief from the pocket of his jeans, and thrust it into her hand.

'The sooner you go back to England, Claire, the better,' he declared. 'You're nothing but a distraction—and one I can well do without!'

Turning, he strode briskly away, leaving her a battlefield of mixed emotions. His compassionate understanding had explained her to herself, freeing her at last from the fear and guilt she had buried deep within her for so long. But in their place he had filled her with unsatisfied longings he had no intention of fulfilling. She loved him and wanted to be part of his life, and he would not let her. What had he called her? A distraction. That was all she was to him.

Claire sniffed and blew her nose. What was to become of this new woman he had made of her, who had finally found a man she could love, and a worthwhile life she could lead? All she had now was the bitter knowledge that neither could be hers. The only thing left for her to do was to put on a brave face and bow out gracefully.

CHAPTER NINE

THEY camped overnight at Tomas's farm and set off on the return journey early the next morning, as soon as Ashley had checked that mother and child were doing well.

Maria-Elena smiled shyly at Claire and presented her with a beautiful shawl she had spun and knitted herself, a 'thank you' for her help.

'Oh, but I didn't do very much,' Claire protested, deeply touched, her limited command of Spanish deserting her. The young woman merely smiled and pressed the gift insistently into her hands. Claire accepted it gladly, knowing she would always treasure it as a memento of her time in Rio Negro.

'They're going to call him Juan,' Basil, who had taken photographs of the new baby, promising to send prints, informed the others as they rode out, waving farewells.

'After Tomas's brother, no doubt,' Ashley said, and Basil's face broke into a grin.

'Hell, no! After *you* ... or so I gathered, although I might have got it wrong. I don't understand Spanish too well. It does say "A.J. Wade" on your doc's bag, so the middle name's John, right?'

'Right.' Ashley's answer was terse and short, and he rode on ahead of them so that they could not see his face. Claire knew he was moved, but did not want to show it.

This she understood, but he seemed equally ashamed of that moment of weakness last night, when he had almost gathered her into his arms and kissed her. She knew he was trying to avoid her as much as possible, speaking to her only when he had to, and very briefly, refusing even to look at her directly.

His attitude made her deeply unhappy. Would it have cost him so dearly to be pleasant during these last hours of their association? Since she could not have his love, she would have settled for the memory of his friendship. But he appeared determined to drive a wedge between them, and any overtures of conversation were met with a polite stone-walling technique that was a rebuff in itself.

It was late when they made camp, and they were all too tired to do more than prepare and eat a makeshift meal before turning in. Ashley sloshed the remains of his coffee on the fire and rolled into his sleeping-bag with a brief 'goodnight', and Claire understood that he intended there to be no campfire chats for the two of them tonight.

But she could not accept this ignominious ending to their partnership. She preferred angry words—and heaven knew there had been plenty between them—to this silent cold-shouldering. Steeling her nerve, she waited until Basil and Greg had retired to their tent, on the pretext of finishing her coffee, and quietly addressed the still figure in the sleeping-bag.

'Just tell me one thing, Ashley, and I'll be satisfied,' she whispered. 'What have I done?'

He rolled over to face her, propping up his chin on his elbow.

'Go to bed, Claire. It's late, and I'm tired.'

'We're all tired. But you owe me an explanation,' she persisted. 'You've treated me like a pariah all day. Is it because of last night…at the farmhouse? Can't we forget what happened when we were both under a strain, and simply be friends?'

'Friends?' he queried coldly. 'Nay, lass, that's asking a bit much. You've done your job, and it's finished. You'll be leaving soon. I'm staying here. That's all there is to it. So push off to bed, and let me get some sleep.'

Later, she knew she was going to hurt badly when she remembered those terse words. But for now, a blessed, all-conquering anger was her salvation. She jumped up, turning her mug upside-down so that the dregs of the coffee formed a muddy puddle on the ground.

'Oh, to hell with it, then!' she exclaimed disgustedly. 'I realised the first time I met you that you hadn't any manners, and nothing that's happened since has revised my opinion!'

Turning her back on him, she stalked off indignantly to her tent.

It took Claire a long time to fall asleep, and then it seemed that she had scarcely closed her eyes before something woke her. The 'something' sounded like a muffled, sickening thud, followed by a grunt of pain, and at first she thought these noises belonged to some weird nightmare she was having. But then she heard soft, scuffling noises, like stealthy footsteps, and suddenly she was wide awake and alert, aware of their lonely vulnerability out here in the middle of nowhere, in the dead of night.

'Ashley?' she queried softly, sitting up and feeling for the flap of her tent, so that she could peer out. But, when she did, she found herself looking straight at a pair of men's legs, not three feet away from her...long legs, clad in heavy, good-quality denim, the feet encased in black leather ankle-boots she had seen none of her companions wearing.

Her horrified gaze travelled upwards, and now she wished it *were* a nightmare, for she was gazing up into a face she recognised, the face of a young man she had seen first on the bus to Aguas Calientes, then in the hotel dining-room, and most recently with Pilar's daughter in San Stefano.

It wasn't his face which worried her. It was the ominous click that drew her attention to the glinting barrel of the revolver in his hand, now pointing directly at her.

'You don't say nothing, *señorita*,' he said softly, in accented but very understandable English. 'You come out of there real slow, and only move when I say you move—OK?'

At first, this advice was quite unnecessary, for Claire was unable to move at all. She had never before been in a life-threatening situation, facing the muzzle of a gun, and she was paralysed with fear, her throat dry, her limbs useless. But he was still pointing the weapon at her, and slowly she got a grip on herself. As she emerged from the tent, she saw the prone figure of Ashley, lying face downward on the floor, two men standing over him, and knew with a dreadful flash of intuition what had caused the thud and the grunt she had heard earlier.

Anxiety for him briefly overcame her fear for herself, and she gasped out accusingly, 'What have you done to him?' She made as if to run to his side, but the man jerked the gun warningly, indicating that she should stay where she was.

'I tell you not move. He OK—just don't take orders too good,' he said darkly, and relief swept over Claire as she watched Ashley struggling to a sitting position, rubbing his head, obviously still dazed from the blow he had been struck.

One of the men guarding him was the other of the two Claire had seen in Aguas Calientes. The third she did not recognise, but he looked easily the meanest of the three, she decided with a shiver, tall, lean, with a drooping moustache and narrow eyes. All three were armed, and she supposed they were about to be robbed. She herself had very little actual cash on her, and only a few of her traveller's cheques left. She had planned a visit to the bank as soon as they arrived back in town. She didn't know how Basil and Greg were fixed, but all of them had been warned by the consular authorities not to carry more than they actually needed. Was it worth these men's while? Will they shoot us if it isn't? she thought, panic-stricken. Will they shoot us, anyway?'

'What the devil's going on out here?'

Greg's face, still dazed with sleep, peered out from the tent, and the mean-looking individual strode over and gave the canvas sides a kick.

'Out of there, you *hombres*!' he commanded sharply, and Basil and Greg crawled out, bewilderment changing to horror on their faces as they looked around them.

Claire had to admire Greg.

'Would you mind telling me what all this is about?' he demanded coldly of the tall man, in his best, most authoritative boardroom manner.

'You'll find out soon enough,' was the growling reply. He turned to the younger man who was guarding Claire. 'Paco—leave the *chica* alone. Get their mules saddled up, and bring ours,' he rapped out, swiftly switching to Spanish.

By this time, Ashley had regained his senses, and struggled to his feet. Claire could see the stickiness of blood in the dark hair at his crown, and his eyes were still dull with pain. But, with a tremendous effort, he faced the leader and made an attempt to reason with him.

'Look—this isn't worth your time and trouble,' he said, in a level, peaceable tone. 'Everyone knows that I haven't two *pesos* to scratch together, and my friends are all foreigners—English. There will be one hell of a stink if anything happens to them, and none of them is carrying much money.'

'Shut up!' the tall man snarled in response, clearly not at all swayed by this argument.

The mules were brought, ready saddled, together with their own which they must have left some way back to make their approach quieter. This was obviously not a random robbery, Claire thought, deeply uneasy. These men had known they would be here, and where to find them. Who had told them? Maria-Elena and Tomas? Any of the people Ashley had treated on the way up? It was unthinkable, but threatened by armed men, she realised that whatever gratitude they owed Ashley people would protect themselves and their families first.

They were allowed to take virtually nothing with them; their tents and luggage left as they were, they were ordered roughly to get on their mules.

'All right.' Ashley had not given up, and Claire was cold with fear for him. 'But can't I take my bag— doctor's bag? Something for my head—OK?'

It was bleeding quite badly, and looked rather a mess, but Claire did not expect this request to be granted, all the same. However, the leader had turned away, and the young man called Paco appeared to have a more casual approach.

'OK—you take bag. Nothing else,' he said, surprisingly, and Claire breathed more easily. As they mounted up, Ashley's leg brushed against hers, warm and reassuring, and his eyes glinted a warning.

'Don't push it—right? These are dangerous men,' he muttered under his breath.

'Take your own advice—you're the one taking risks!' she hissed back, angry with relief.

'Man, I won't even breathe!' Basil declared, shaking his head. 'No one told me this trip was likely to get so hairy!'

'No talk!' Paco drawled threateningly. 'Quiet! Ride!'

He brought up the rear behind them as they rode down the trail. A sickle moon swung in the sky above them, brightening their path, but the hills were dark and silent.

If they had wanted to rob and kill us, they would surely have done so by now, Claire reasoned hopefully. There must be something else they wanted. What? She wished she knew where they were being taken.

Not to San Stefano, that was certain, for she recognised the point where the trail led off in that direction. Instead, they followed a much narrower path which plunged downhill into a steep valley, thickly covered with thorny trees which snagged at her legs as they rode. The track petered out often, and then they picked it up again, and she guessed that it was very little used.

After they had been riding silently for several hours, they came to a small clearing in the woods. There was a stone-built cottage, and obviously someone was already here, for a mule was tethered outside. Claire could hear the trickle of water, indicating that there must be a stream nearby.

'It looks as if it was once a charcoal-burner's cottage,' Ashley said quietly in her ear. 'Long abandoned by the original inhabitant, most likely. But we are expected. This was set up.'

'But why? What do they want with us?' she muttered back.

'I've got my suspicions,' he replied grimly. Then he smiled at her, a ghost of his usual jaunty grin, but in these circumstances it was worth more to her than gold. 'Chin up, Claire. Don't let them see we're scared.'

They all dismounted, as they were roughly ordered to do, and then they were herded towards the cottage. Paco kicked the door with the toe of his leather boot, and they heard the sound of bolts being drawn back.

It was still dark. The trees all around cast deep shadows, and the interior of the hut was lit only by a single feeble lantern. But there was no doubt as to the identity of the girl who opened the door, the swirl of her red skirt, and the defiant flash of her dark eyes. It was Yolanda.

'"*Et tu, Brute*,"' Ashley murmured softly. The quotation obviously meant nothing to the girl, but she understood the soft reproach of his accusation, for she pouted and turned her back, flouncing outside, closely followed by Paco, who pinched her bottom lightly.

The door was closed on the four of them and, alone, they stared at each other in the faint glow of the lantern. Although the door had no lock, only the bolts which closed it from within, they were all too aware of the three armed men outside. There was no escape that way. The cottage had two small windows, but these were heavily shuttered and barred. There were a few blankets cast about on the floor, and a trestle table on which stood boxes of provisions. In one corner stood a portable stove of the kind Claire had often used on Girl Guide camping holidays, complete with a canister of bottled gas.

'It's not exactly the Holiday Inn,' Greg said drily, 'but it would seem our...er...visit has been provided for.'

'It's obviously all been arranged,' Ashley agreed. 'Pilar knew where we were going, and when, and Yolanda must have got the information from her to pass on to her friends. You were right, Claire, about that young fellow hanging around San Stefano. It wasn't as innocent as it seemed.'

Claire felt as if somewhere back along the line a shoe had dropped, and she had been waiting ever since for the second one to fall.

'Not only in San Stefano,' she said slowly. 'They were watching us in Aguas Calientes . . . two of them were on the bus which brought us there. All this was planned.'

Basil flopped down on to one of the blankets, leaning back against the wall.

'I don't believe this is happening!' he exclaimed. 'We've been kidnapped! We're hostages. But none of us is wealthy. Could it be political?'

Before any of them could answer, the door opened again, and the moustachioed leader slipped inside. They all tensed, recognising that the danger emanated from him. The other two would do as he told them, but all of them sensed that he would personally kill them, without compunction, if it served his purpose.

Keeping one hand on his gun, he drew a piece of paper and a ballpoint pen from his pocket and tossed them to the ground at Greg's feet.

'You!' he snarled, cold but menacing. 'Write your company. Tell them your life is in great danger. Tell them we shoot you all if our demands are not met!'

Greg picked up the paper and pen slowly, and hesitated as he looked at the other three.

'Write it,' Ashley said. 'I didn't take this lot for political idealists of any kind—they're straightforwardly mercenary. You don't have any choice—unless any of us has a burning desire to be a dead hero.'

Looking their captor directly in the eye, he said clearly, 'My friend will do as you have told him to, but have you thought this through? His company is big and powerful, and employs many people in Rio Negro. If it closes down factories or pulls out because of this, they will be without jobs. Many will suffer and go hungry.'

The kidnapper regarded him stonily, and gave a contemptuous shrug. Clearly, he was no altruist.

'They will pay—that is all I care—doctor!' he sneered. 'They will pay—or *you* will.'

Greg wrote the letter, managing somehow to keep his hand steady, Claire noted admiringly. She was proud of the way all three of her companions were keeping their nerve under pressure, even Basil, who a short time ago had found it hard to get through the day without a bottle. She was determined not to let the side down.

'The man to whom you should send this is B.J. Lawson,' Greg said, clearly and precisely. 'He is managing director for South American operations, and is the only one with the authority to do what you ask.'

He handed over the note, and after scanning it swiftly the kidnapper gave a curt nod.

'Now your passport,' he demanded. 'So this Señor Lawson, he knows we really do have you, and we mean business.'

Greg unzipped the pouch in his belt where he kept his documents, and withdrew the slim blue folder, surrendering it without a word. Then once again the door was closed on them, and they were alone.'

'This guy, Lawson,' Basil queried nervously. 'Will he pay up?'

Greg made a forced attempt at a smile.

'I don't know how much they're asking for our safe release, but we have to hope Brian Lawson thinks I'm worth it,' he said. 'Seriously, I don't see what else the company can do. It would be very bad for its image to allow executives to be shot out of hand. Who would want to work for an organisation which wasn't prepared to look after its own?'

'But it might be equally bad for its image to be seen to have given in to blackmail. It could start a chain of such kidnappings wherever General Chemicals operates,' Claire pointed out quietly, and they all looked at her soberly, weighing the impact of her words.

'They can't just abandon us to our fate,' Greg said reassuringly. 'I'm well paid, but this kind of risk isn't written into my contract! We just have to sit tight, behave ourselves, and let Brian sort it out.'

Ashley did not comment, and Claire could tell from the doubtful expression in his eyes that he was not entirely in accord with this sentiment.

'Still want to play doctor, Ms Mallory?' he asked. 'They made a real mess of my head. Bring my bag, and see what we can find.'

Using some of the drinking water from the container provided, trusting that it was clean and uncontaminated, since their captors would be drinking it, too, Claire carefully cleaned the sticky mess of congealed blood from Ashley's dark hair, and applied astringent.

'Ouch!' he complained. 'That stings! You're hurting me!'

'Be quiet, and don't moan. Everyone knows that doctors make the worst possible patients,' she told him.

She was very close to him, and had to fight a strong desire to put her arms round him and hold him to her. What did all their arguments matter, now, when their lives were on the line? He must have shared her thoughts, for he looked up at her, the grin fading from his face, and he held her gaze very thoughtfully and seriously.

'I hate myself for getting you into this,' he said, so quietly that only she could hear his words.

Claire swallowed hard. Careful, she told herself, he's only concerned for your safety—nothing more.

'Didn't you tell me it was futile to blame oneself for something one couldn't prevent?' she asked. Lowering her voice even further, she added, 'You aren't so sanguine about our hopes of getting out of this, are you? You don't think they're going to let us go, even when they have the money?'

'I think it's going to be very difficult for General Chemicals' management to enforce its conditions,' he replied carefully. 'And I wouldn't give these chaps ten out of ten for trustworthiness. They've taken no precautions to conceal their identities from us—no masks over their faces, for instance, and Yolanda is well known to us. In a sense, it's a very amateurish operation, and that makes me uneasy.'

Claire's heart felt like a cold, heavy lump of rock weighted in her breast, but not performing its proper function. This could not be happening to her, an ordinary English girl. Her life could not really be in this awful danger. It was so unreal that she could scarcely grasp it, so horrible that her mind refused fully to take it in.

'Then we have to find a way to escape from them,' she whispered urgently. 'We can't just sit here and wait for them to kill us. At least we have to give ourselves a chance of survival.'

His hand was warm and steady on hers.

'My sentiments exactly,' he agreed. 'Every problem has a solution, somewhere, if one can only find it. Think on—as my mother always said, whenever she came up against something puzzling. I'm thinking. Try and rest, Claire. Exhaustion won't help us any. If a chance comes, we have to be alert enough to take it.'

She knew he was right but, tired as they all were, they could do no more than doze fitfully. Later in the morning, Paco and Yolanda came in, and she boiled up some thin, tasteless soup on the camping stove, teasing and flirting with the young man all the while, rolling her huge eyes and swivelling her hips suggestively.

Through the half-open door, they could see the other man on guard, but there was no sign of the moustachioed one.

'Where's your leader?' Ashley asked casually, as Paco handed out rough hunks of bread.

'Carlos gone to city.' He rubbed his fingers and thumb together in a braggart gesture. '*Mucho dinero*. We rich soon,' he boasted, grinning.

Ashley grinned back. 'What will you do with all that money? You'll have to leave Rio Negro, of course. Go to Rio de Janeiro? You can have a good time there. Nice beaches, nightclubs, lots of good-looking *chicas... muy lindas!*'

Yolanda flashed him a resentful glance, not liking the bit about the Brazilian girls, but Paco licked his lips appreciatively. His gaze flicked over Claire, admiring the loosely tumbled blonde locks.

'This one very nice!' he said meaningfully, and Claire shuddered.

Ashley slipped a proprietorial arm round her shoulder.

'This one mine,' he said easily. Captive and captor faced one another for a moment. On the surface of it, Paco had the upper hand—he was armed, and there was nothing to stop him doing as he pleased with Claire, if he was determined to. On the other hand, he had an easy-going nature which avoided trouble, and, since most of San Stefano believed that Claire was Ashley's woman, he probably didn't doubt it. Shrugging his shoulders, he turned and strolled out of the hut, closely followed by a furious Yolanda.

'There you are—I knew one day you'd be grateful for that piece of fiction,' Ashley said to Claire, with just a glint of humour in his eyes. 'Believe it or not, there are worse fates than my attentions.'

A lot of water had flowed under the bridge since she had found that notion distasteful—if, indeed, she ever had—but even without Greg and Basil's listening ears this was hardly the time or the place for a confession of love.

Outside, they could hear the voices of Paco and Yolanda, hers sulky and pleading by turns, his cajoling...then soft laughter and murmurs which suggested he had placated her.

'She didn't take too kindly to what you said about other women,' Greg pointed out uneasily. 'I don't think it's wise to stir them up.'

'It may be our only hope,' Ashley contradicted. 'Divide and rule.'

'Our only hope is for Greg's company to shell out the money,' Basis said. A sudden silence fell among them. They were all aware of how great was the danger. But, although he said nothing more, Claire was convinced that Ashley had some purpose in mind, towards which he was working.

The afternoon was endless. To keep their spirits up, they talked, each recounting funny anecdotes from their past, describing childhood days, recalling favourite places, films, books, restaurants—anything to take their minds several thousand miles away from a deserted hut in a forest clearing, guarded by ruffians.

When it grew dark, Yolanda reappeared and started to prepare some sort of evening meal. They could hear the voices of the two men outside, see the glow of their cigarette ends through the crack in the door, enticingly left open. Escape seemed so close, but tantalisingly impossible when they reminded themselves that their guards were armed and dangerous, and there was no getting away without overpowering them and reaching the mules.

Ashley stood up, stretched, and casually leaned against the wall, watching Yolanda as she chopped onions. She looked at him suspiciously, a little shamefacedly, and he smiled at her, a friendly, open smile, free of recrimination.

'You like Paco?' he asked, addressing her in her own language, his voice pleasant, level, and without a hint of accusation. She glanced at him out of the corner of her eye and went on chopping the onions, declining to answer him. 'Yes, I can see you do,' he went on. 'He's a good-looking young man. I expect he knows how to give a girl a good time. Promised to take you to Brazil or somewhere, has he, buy you lots of nice clothes, stay in fancy hotels, huh? You're a pretty girl, Yolanda.'

Despite herself, it was obvious her vanity was flattered, and she allowed him an arch little smile, patting her hair self-consciously.

'But there are lots of pretty girls.' His tone had changed subtly, there was a touch of scorn in it, and a warning, too. 'Why should Paco take you along? We have a saying in my country, "you don't take coals to Newcastle". It means, why take with you something that's already plentiful where you are going?'

Yolanda scowled and looked down, biting her lip. Claire, following this monologue as well as she could, realised that even now, with their circumstances so changed, Ashley still presented to the girl a figure of authority—doctor, foreigner, employer—and she could not quite shake off this image.

Ashley picked up a piece of raw onion from the table and popped it into his mouth, chewing appreciatively and swallowing it.

'They'll leave you behind, you know, one way or another,' he said confidingly. 'Why should they share the money with you? You'll be the one who goes to prison, while they are on the beach at Copacabana.'

She rounded on him at last, eyes spitting resentment.

'It's not true!' she declared defiantly.

Ashley shrugged.

'No? You know, I think you may be right,' he said. 'You won't go to prison, because Carlos will take the money and kill us all—me, my friends, and you, Yolanda. After all, *you* know who he is. He can never come home while you're alive, can he? *Qué lástima!* What a pity!'

She glared at him speechlessly, then flung down the knife and stalked out of the cottage, slamming the door furiously behind her.

'That's some hell-cat!' Basil exclaimed nervously. 'I didn't catch half of what you said, but you were obviously winding her up! Man, you'll get us killed!'

'I don't think so,' Ashley said imperturbably. 'Paco and friend won't do anything until Carlos gets back, and they know whether he's managed to make a deal with General Chemicals. And Yolanda might just be our salvation. Don't you see? Underneath all that swagger, she's just a frightened kid who's been sucked into something too big for her. These desperadoes have simply used her, and sooner or later they're going to unload her.'

Almost on cue, the sounds of an argument reached their ears. Yolanda's voice was sullen and accusing to begin with, and Paco was non-committal, refusing to be drawn. But as her anger increased, her shouts rising to a pitch of screaming invective, he began to respond to her with taunts and insults.

Was she mad? Of course he couldn't take an ignorant little peasant like her to a great city like Rio de Janeiro. She'd show him up. Why, she probably wouldn't know which knife and fork to use in a restaurant, and anyhow, there'd be no shortage of prettier, classier girls—especially when you had pockets full of money.

They listened breathlessly as Ashley translated some of these insults for their benefit. Yolanda was crying now, hysterical and out of control. There was the sound of a ringing slap, flat of hand against tender skin, then a rough command to shut up and get on with cooking dinner. The door was opened and the girl catapulted inside, obviously pushed from behind, to fall in a sobbing, wailing heap on the floor at their feet.

Claire gazed down at Yolanda's heaving shoulders and tumbled black hair. The girl had led the kidnappers to them, sold them for a price, but, strangely, she did not bear her any ill will. She had seen what it was like to be grindingly poor, and could imagine how it felt to know that youth and prettiness were all one had...and only fleetingly. And then, to be offered an escape, promised riches and pleasure and fun, the chance to *live* a little...could *she* have been strong enough to turn down such a stroke of fortune, if she had been Yolanda?

Looking up at Ashley, she said, 'Well, she knows now that Paco was only using her. You've taught her a lesson, and she's one of us now, but how is she—how are any of us going to profit from it?'

A slow smile teased his mouth as he knelt and lifted the sobbing girl, a comforting arm round her slim shoulders. 'She's going to help us,' he said. 'To save her own skin...for revenge...to name but two motives. And I've worked out precisely how she's going to do it.'

His smile widened out into a broad, optimistic grin.

'Dinner is going to be a little late tonight,' he said. 'But our friends out there are going to have the pleasure of an extra course they hadn't bargained on!'

Yolanda was young, vain and featherbrained, but even so a native intelligence allowed her to understand what her fate must be unless she took a hand in changing it. Paco had led her on with promises he had no intention of keeping, and when she had hastily rushed into confronting him with the doubts Ashley had stirred up, he was too hot-headed and arrogant to bother stringing her along with more lies. So far as he was concerned, she had served her purpose.

She had not really understood what they had planned to do with the doctor and the other foreigners. All Paco had told her, apparently, was that if she divulged where they were going, helped look after them, did a bit of cooking, she would be well rewarded. But now it was all too plain to her what was really in store for all of them when Carlos got back, and she was badly scared.

It was fairly easy for Ashley to persuade her that her one hope lay in helping them to get away before that happened, and the fact that she had helped them would stand her in good stead when the kidnappers were caught and brought to justice. She could plead ignorance, foolishness and a willingness to turn state's evidence. But first they all had to get out of here, and that meant dealing with Paco and the other man. That was where her part came in.

'Our two friends,' Ashley said drily to Claire, 'are going to have a bout of iatrogenic disease . . . which, literally translated, means "sickness caused by the doctor".'

Her brow puckered, then cleared.

'I get it. You're going to put something in their coffee?'

'I hope it isn't poison,' Greg said cautiously. 'We're in dire straits, but I don't fancy being an accessory to murder, even so.'

Ashley shook his head.

'What I have in mind won't kill them. In normal doses, it's used as a sedative, and even the amount that I...that is to say, Yolanda, will give them, will only make them have a nice long sleep. Long enough for us to get away from here. Are we all agreed on this? Because quite honestly, I don't see any other way, and I, for one, am not yet ready to be a corpse.'

No one hesitated. Anything was preferable to waiting here and consigning themselves to the doubtful mercy of Carlos. They all nodded instant agreement.

'You told me once that you were helpless without your doctor's bag,' Claire said, suddenly struck by the memory. 'It was back in Aguas Calientes, when you treated the little boy with whooping cough. But I don't think this was quite what you had in mind. We were lucky they let you bring it along.'

'I don't expect it occurred to them that the drugs a doctor uses can serve other than medicinal purposes,' he said. 'It didn't occur to me at the time, either, I must confess. I only knew that without it, I've a sense missing. I didn't know how grateful I was going to be for the drugs I carry about with me.'

Dinner that night, when Yolanda had finally calmed herself enough to prepare it, was a scrawny fowl disguised in a tasteless stew, worthy of her mother's less happy results. It was tough and indigestible, and to Claire, at least, it was obvious that the girl was too nervous to care what she was doing. She was tempted to offer her help, but resisted, knowing that it might arouse suspicion if they appeared too friendly. Everything must appear normal and, if Yolanda had cooked for her companions before, they would not be expecting a great culinary experience. Claire forced herself to eat, knowing they would need all their strength and energy.

It was unbearably stuffy in the tiny cottage, especially with the cooking in progress, so while their prisoners sweltered inside, the two men sat in the doorway in the relative cool of the night, but always one of them had his hand on a gun, ready to dissuade them from any attempt at escape. Yolanda boiled the water for the coffee, her hands trembling badly, and under cover of taking his Ashley slipped her the small bottle into which he had decanted a suitable dose for her to divide between two of the mugs.

'*Ahora*—now,' he said quietly. 'Don't worry—they won't be able to taste it.'

The coffee was certainly harsh and bitter enough to drown the taste of anything in it, Claire thought, hope rising in her as she drank hers. They lolled on their blankets, keeping up the pretence of a discussion of a performance of *Cats*, which Greg and Claire had both seen in London, and about which they had differing opinions. Yolanda crouched, shivering with fear, her eyes darting to the door every now and then. They had closed it now, but those indoors could hear the two of them laughing, sharing a bottle of *aguardiente*.

'Alcohol should help the process along nicely,' Ashley said with satisfaction.

It didn't happen all at once. The talk began to grow more desultory, and there was a slurred quality about it. They heard Paco berating his companion, whose turn it was to keep watch first, and who loudly denied that he'd been falling asleep. Then for a long time there was no sound at all, and they began to fret with impatience because Ashley made them wait a further half-hour, calculating the effect of the drug with an eye on his watch.

'Man, let's go before it starts to wear off!' Basil begged. 'What are we waiting for?'

'It's our one chance. If we fluff it, we won't get another,' Ashley said grimly. 'I want those two cowboys well and truly in the arms of Morpheus before we make a move.'

At last he decided it was safe enough to risk it, and opened the door cautiously. The night was silent. Paco was rolled up in his sleeping-bag, eyes closed, confident that his friend was on guard. But he was slumped against the wall, his head bent almost to his knees, oblivious of everything. For all that, they crept out very quietly, making their way stealthily to where the mules were tethered.

'We'll take theirs, too, for good measure,' Ashley said. 'Even when they come round, they won't get far in pursuit of us on foot. All we have to do now is to find our way back to San Stefano.'

It wasn't easy. They had ridden the elusive track only once before, under guard, and worrying about their personal safety rather than the route. Even Yolanda, who knew it slightly better, was of little help, and kept leading them round in circles, then bursting into tears because they were lost, and Carlos would come back and kill them before they even got out of the forest.

'Carlos will not return so quickly,' Ashley reassured her gently, and with a depth of patience that took Claire by surprise. She was still learning about the resources this man could draw on from within himself, when he needed to. 'He has to go to the capital and somehow contact Señor Telford's company, without giving himself away. It will take time. Think, Yolanda—do we turn left here, or right?'

The sun was breaking splendidly through the dispersing night clouds as they picked up the trail to San Stefano. All of them breathed a little more easily, but they did not relax, and stopped for only a short rest en route. Tired, dusty, hungry, and yet full of an immense relief and thankfulness, they saw at last the stone walls of the doctor's house awaiting them like a haven, and to Claire this simple dwelling suddenly assumed a mantle of homeliness and welcome.

She no longer shuddered at its rough, makeshift appearance, or thought with horror of its primitive facilities. Now she saw its sturdy walls as a refuge of peace, the struggling vegetable patch as a symbol of one man's fierce endeavour, the door to the surgery representing hope for and faith in the future. The huddled houses of the village in the distance, full of people she had come to know a little, and sympathise with, the rugged, towering mountains and the hot skies inspired her with a strange affection.

It felt like home. Sliding off her mule, she met the tired, rakish, triumphant blue gaze of Ashley Wade, and the love she had for him rose up overpoweringly, so that she was sure it must be shining from her eyes and radiating from every pore of her skin. It was a moment so emotional that she almost sensed the air between them quivering. If only she could reach out to him now, abandon pretence and tell him how she felt, throw her love at his feet and tell him it was his for the taking...

'Ashley...' she began, hesitant but still brimming over with feeling.

He put a hand briefly over hers where it lay on the saddle.

'Claire—don't say anything,' he said warningly. 'We've been through a lot together, and we'd be inhuman if it hadn't affected us. But it's over now, so let it go. OK?'

They had only a moment alone, apart from the others, and it was impossible for Claire to cram into that brief space all she was thinking and feeling. His eyes, his manner, were holding up a barrier, warning her that he preferred not to know. She could not force her love upon a man who did not want it. She could only accept her loss with good grace, go her way, and let him go his.

'All right, Ashley. If that's the way you want it,' she made herself agree quietly.

'Aye, lass. That's the way I want it,' he confirmed.

His answer was firm and unequivocal, leaving no room for doubt, and Claire shrugged and turned away, pretending to see to her mule, but in truth so that he would not see the tears hovering importunately on her lashes.

CHAPTER TEN

BEING back in England again was very strange. Claire found it difficult to accustom herself to streets full of prosperous, well-clothed, well-fed-looking citizens, to toilets that flushed and electric lights that switched on and off with instant obedience. Her flat seemed large and luxurious, over-furnished and over-equipped for one lone female who did not spend much time in it. The restaurants and cinemas and shops made her blink at the sight of so many people extravagantly in pursuit of pleasure.

She was as badly disorientated now as she had been on first arriving in Central America. And the effect did not wear off as easily as the jet lag.

No one else seemed to be similarly affected. Basil, when she met him at the *World Focus* office for a meeting with Harold about the article, appeared relaxed and happy to be back.

'Sure was one hell-hole, that Rio Negro,' he whistled. 'Man, if it weren't for Ashley and that clever trick with the coffee, we'd all most likely be good and dead! I don't mind admitting I was glad to see the back of that place!'

Claire smiled, pleased to see that he had ordered mineral water with lunch.

'But your pictures are fantastic...absolutely stunning,' she said. 'Don't you feel ... well, a little nostalgic when you look at them?'

'Hell, no!' he said fervently.

Greg expressed much the same sentiments.

167

'I'm glad I went,' he said. 'It made me understand what people like Ashley are trying to do, what he's up against, and I admire him for it. But rather him than me, that's all I can say. I'll do as much as I can to help, but strictly from this end!'

So it was only she, Claire, who nursed this fugitive tug of affection for the poor mountain village in its remote, savagely beautiful setting. It wasn't simply that she loved Ashley. She could have fallen in love with him while continuing to hate San Stefano. The hard but ironic truth was that she now asked nothing better than to do the very thing she would have feared a short time ago— to stay at the side of the man she loved, and help those most in need. But he had not wanted her.

Those last hours in Rio Negro had passed in a daze. After a short rest, they had ridden into Aguas Calientes and presented themselves to the *Comisaría* to explain what had happened to them. The questioning they had endured seemed endless and frustrating, and at first Claire suspected that the chief of police thought these four crazy foreigners were making up the entire story. Yolanda, who could do nothing but weep copiously and protest that she hadn't understood what was going on, was not much help either. But Greg's insistence on a phone call to General Chemicals' headquarters in Rio Negro, and the authoritative confirmation of Brian Lawson, finally persuaded them that it was not all an imaginative fabrication.

With the hostages safe, and no fear of reprisals being taken, it had been fairly easy to trap Carlos into arranging a meeting to collect his ransom money, and with him singing like a bird about his co-conspirators, Claire imagined they would soon be rounded up, too.

This time, there was no rickety bus ride into the capital, but the offer—indeed, the insistence—of a police escort in an armoured car.

'Brian,' Greg said with satisfaction, 'has been creating an almighty fuss in high places about the safety of his executive personnel. We get VIP treatment until we leave the country. We depart first thing in the morning. Meanwhile, we have the delights of the Hotel Principal for the night, and that includes you, Ashley. I therefore have pleasure in inviting all of you to a celebration dinner.'

They had the best rooms in the hotel put at their disposal, by order of *el jefe*, the police chief. Claire could not repress an ironic smile when she discovered that hers was nothing less than the bridal chamber. Still, the shower was working, even if it only ran cold water, and she let it stream all over her body until she finally felt clean, surveying in the mirror her body, sunburned and browned in parts, still palely white in others, like a patchwork quilt.

She had just stepped out of the shower, her hair still wringing wet, when there was a tap on the door of her bedroom.

'Who is it?' she called, wrapping a towel sarong-wise around herself.

'Claire.' The voice was unmistakably Ashley's, brisk and peremptory. 'I want to speak to you. It won't take more than a minute.'

She went weak at the knees, her body all a-shiver with strange sensations. There had been a finality in his words on arrival back at San Stefano, but here he was, at her door...and here she was, clad only in a bath towel. A surge of hope and elation crested within her, and she crossed the room swiftly to open the door.

But her hopes died as she saw that he was fully kitted out for travelling—boots, cords, his worn old jacket with its plethora of pockets, wide-brimmed hat, saddlebags on the floor beside him.

'Well, Claire,' he said softly, 'so they gave you the matrimonial bedroom—the one they usually reserve for honeymoon couples. What a waste, for you to occupy it alone.'

It was impossible to tell whether he was serious or joking. Claire swallowed hard, feeling cold inside.

'You're leaving,' she said flatly.

He said, 'I've changed my plans. If I'm here tomorrow, I know I'll get shoved into that car with the rest of you and carted off to the capital,' he said. 'There will be more questions, more time wasted. I can't afford it. I've patients who haven't seen me for the best part of a week as it is. If I push off now, quietly, I'll be half-way to San Stefano before anyone realises I've gone.'

Claire thought her heart actually stopped for a moment. She could not feel the reassuring regularity of its healthy beat, and had to wait for it to start up again before she could speak.

'So this is it—goodbye? Just like that?' she said, with ill-concealed despair. 'You're walking out, and I won't see you again. I'm surprised you bothered to tell me.'

He said, 'I *had* to. And it doesn't make it any easier to find you standing there dripping all over the floor, and revealing damn near everything.'

His voice was full of raw reluctance, and she could feel him palpably resisting temptation.

'Then stay, Ashley,' she said quietly.

His intent blue eyes moved from Claire to the bed, and then back to her once again.

'Believe me, lass,' he told her, and now there wasn't a hint of jest discernible in his voice. 'there's nothing I'd like better. But I can't. So cheerio.'

The square outside was in darkness, so she did not see him leave. Only the quiet clop of Modesta's hoofs on the cobbles testified to the awful fact that he had gone.

Should she have flung aside the towel and thrown herself into his arms, begging him to make love to her? she wondered. The kind of woman he had once believed her to be would not have hesitated. But Claire was not that kind of woman. He must know now that she loved him, and if, in spite of that knowledge, he still insisted on walking out on her, then there was nothing more that she could do.

The most Claire could do, to help Ashley, was to write her article to the best of her ability, and she shut herself into her flat and wrote with a fierce, controlled intensity until she was as satisfied with the end product as she could ever be. On finishing it, she felt drained and depleted, but aware of a light-headed exaltation which could have been due to hunger—she had not stopped to eat all day—but was more likely the result of a growing conviction that this was the best work she had done, or would ever do.

Harold Jones shared her enthusiasm when he read the finished article.

'Terrific stuff, Claire,' he said. 'You gave it your best shot, no doubt about that. No one could read this without being intrigued, moved—and enraged. The world's your oyster now, professionally speaking. The only question now is, where do you go from here?'

'On holiday, preferably,' Claire said laconically. She was gratified by his praise, of course, but could not succeed in working up any enthusiasm for future projects. Was this only a temporary reaction to the exhausting Rio Negro trip, or was this the apex of her journalistic career?

It could be that she would never again write with the fervour and commitment she had given to Ashley Wade's mission, and she was surprised how little the prospect troubled her. She was becoming increasingly sure that she no longer wanted to spend the rest of her life researching and writing articles. She was twenty-four, and life stretched ahead, demanding an answer. There must be something she could do which would both fill the aching void in herself, and perform some service for others.

Hadn't she proved at San Stefano that she was not as helpless or inadequate in the face of suffering as she had always believed? She might be unqualified, but she had a lot to give, and there must be other parts of the world crying out for willing hands to do work many did not relish.

And relinquish her affluent life-style—the nice flat, smart clothes, good pay cheques? She would miss them, no doubt. But their importance had shrunk since her Central American trip, and she asked herself seriously if they were enough to sustain her in a purposeless existence. After all, it now looked very much as if marriage and children were to play no part in her life.

She supposed she could find someone else, if she were determined to, but it would be a second-best solution, unfair to herself and to the unfortunate man who had the unenviable task of trying to take the place of Ashley Wade. So she had turned out to be a one-man woman after all, going half-way round the world to make the discovery, only to be dismissed as an irrelevance.

Claire took some time off, locked up her flat and drove down to Sussex to the haunts of her childhood, hoping to find peace and quiet, ease for her pain, and a measure of inspiration about her future. The seaside resorts were jumping with visitors, now summer had arrived, but she avoided them and walked the green, sweeping downs, with distant views of the sea, and found plenty of solitude there. In the small village where her father had once run his practice, she even found people who remembered her as a lanky schoolgirl.

'Always thought you'd end up being a doctor, like your Dad,' said the motherly landlady at the inn where she stayed. 'He used to tell people that one day your name would be on the brass plaque alongside his—he was convinced of it. But there you are—we can't always do what our parents want us to do, can we? Mine would have liked me to teach, but I just haven't got it up here.' She grinned, tapping her forehead philosophically.

Claire smiled back. Not so long ago, those words would have induced a rush of bitterness and guilt, but she had come to terms now, with what she'd been wont to think of as her failure. Ashley had done that for her, at least.

'If you can run this place, you can't be short of anything "up there",' she rejoined. 'Most of us are capable of far more than we know, and we don't realise it until fate gives us the chance of finding out.'

The landlady gave her a puzzled frown, and went on laying the tables for lunch.

'Well, I'm sure you know what you're talking about,' she said doubtfully. 'Fate gave me my Harry, and the Green Man, and I'm happy to be stuck with both of them. A good man's half the battle won, you know—if you can find him!'

'Yes, I know,' Claire agreed quietly.

If you could find him. And if, having found him, he wanted you in return. Idly, she picked up the copy of

that morning's newspaper which was lying on the bar,
and glanced down at the headlines.

They jumped up, shrieking at her and grabbing her
by the throat. Alarm and fear coursed through her, as
she forced herself to calm down and read on.

> 'COUP D'ETAT OUSTS RULING FACTION
> There was fierce street fighting and some damage
> to property in the Central American republic of
> Rio Negro yesterday as a group of young army
> officers and intellectuals seized power from the
> military junta which has ruled for the past three
> years, but first reports say that the uprising was
> relatively free of bloodshed...'

The unsteady bounce of her heartbeat slowed as she
read the rest of the report. The capital, according to the
correspondent, was now quiet but tense, and life was
returning to normal. Looters would be shot on sight,
but there would be no kangaroo courts or unlawful
killings, the new rulers insisted. The country deserved a
new deal, and they promised free elections and a return
to civilian rule as soon as this could be effected...

Claire closed her eyes and tried hard to picture the
sleazy, run-down city she had passed through briefly.
She imagined it with buildings on fire, rioters in the
streets, soldiers exchanging fire and bullets crackling.

But that was in the capital, she told herself. Presumably the smaller provincial cities would also feel the
effects of the coup. But out in the country, in the vast,
remote hinterland, surely there, nothing much would
have happened? There would be no looting and rioting
in the dusty alleys of San Stefano...would there? Ashley
would not be threatened.

Claire itched with impatience until it was time for the
lunch-time television news, then she promptly switched

on the set in her room. But the footage shown of the country's disturbed capital told her nothing she did not already know. It looked relatively calm, as if the worst were over, but how could she ever know real peace of mind without being sure that Ashley was safe? She picked up the telephone and called the only person she knew who might be able to help her.

'Claire!' Greg Telford's voice was surprised and pleased. 'I saw Harold Jones the other day, and was asking after you. He said you'd gone off on holiday, and were totally incommunicado. Where are you—Outer Mongolia?'

'No. Cast adrift in deepest Sussex,' she replied. 'But not so far adrift that I haven't heard the news. This thing in Rio Negro—I suppose you know about it?'

'Indeed. Lucky for us we managed to miss out on it,' he laughed. 'I consider we had quite enough in the way of excitement, without getting mixed up in a revolution! Let's hope this new government means what it says, and some improvement comes about. I'm still waiting for a final board decision on the proposals I submitted, but...'

Claire cut him off with an impatience which she later realised bordered on rudeness.

'Oh, Greg, never mind that for now! What I want to know is if there has been any news of Ashley? Or have you any way of getting through quickly, to find out if he's safe?'

There was a brief, hesitant silence at the other end of the line.

'Claire, you know it's not possible to communicate directly with San Stefano,' Greg said soothingly. 'There's no telephone in the village, and Ashley even has to pick up his mail in Aguas. But I managed to have a brief word with Brian Lawson this morning, once the phone links were restored. He says things are getting back to normal, and as Central American revolutions go, this one wasn't too bloody.'

Claire's emotional antennae immediately picked up the negative vibrations he was trying to cover up by talking too much, too smoothly.

'That's fine, but it still doesn't tell me whether Ashley is safe or not,' she persisted. 'Greg, I *have* to know.'

She practically heard him shrug.

'I shouldn't worry too much, Claire. Ashley's a survivor. These shoot-outs usually involve the cities—that's where all the action is. Out in the country, I expect things are much quieter. *We* probably learned about the coup before they did in San Stefano.'

Common sense, and her understanding of the workings of the Press told Claire that he might well be right about that. Why, then, did she have this feeling that he was hiding something from her? He sounded too deliberately casual and unworried. It had to be a front for something he did not want her to know.

'That's not the whole story, is it?' she demanded, gripping the receiver tightly, teetering on the edge of hysteria. 'There's something you aren't telling me! Ashley *was* in the city, wasn't he... and he's hurt? Or he's...he's...'

Her voice rose to a pitch she scarcely recognised, until she was virtually screaming down the telephone.

'Greg! Don't play games like this! *You've got to tell me!*'

'Claire!' His voice rapped out sharply. 'Get a grip on yourself! Ashley is safe, I tell you. He's all right.'

'How do you know?' She wasn't satisfied. 'You're simply saying that to shut me up! Greg, tell me the truth! You simply have to! I can't live unless I know!'

He sighed.

'All right, Claire. Calm down, have a drink of water, or a double Scotch, or something. OK?'

He waited until she had composed herself a little, and then went on, resignedly.

'The reason I know that Ashley was not hurt in the trouble in Rio Negro is that he wasn't there. He's here in England, and has been for the past two weeks.'

Claire subsided into a stunned, shocked silence. Then in a small voice she said, 'Here? Why? How *can* he be? I'd have heard...wouldn't I? After all, *you* knew. How come you didn't tell me before?'

This time the sigh was heavier.

'You aren't going to like this, Claire, but here it comes. I didn't tell you because he specifically asked me not to do so. I'm breaking his confidence by telling you now, only because you were so distraught.'

He paused.

'Claire, anyone would have had to be deaf, blind and stupid not to know that something was going on between you two back in Rio Negro. But whatever it was, it's over as far as Ashley is concerned. He told me you were the last person he wanted to see.'

Claire gulped. This was just about the most painful message she had ever received. Ashley was here, in England, and would not even see her. Was he so afraid of her love, so embarrassed by it that he could not bear to face her, even for a casual meeting?

'I'm sorry, Claire.' Greg's voice cut through the fog of her wretchedness. 'I couldn't see any way to put it less brutally, although I wouldn't have wanted to hurt you for the world.'

'No...no. It's not your fault. I'm grateful to you for giving it to me straight,' she assured him miserably. 'But since you've told me this much, surely you can tell me ... how is he? How are things in San Stefano? And when will he be going back?'

'Things were pretty much the same. They rounded up Paco and his mate, and Yolanda is going to get off pretty lightly, on account of having helped us in the end.'

Again she felt his hesitation, and knew he was still holding back. Then he seemed to come to a decision.

'You might as well know the rest. Knowing Ashley, you'll probably have guessed that he isn't here on holiday. He's been very ill.'

He heard her gasp over the phone, and said, 'Take it easy—he's going to be all right. To cut a long story short, he had to go into the capital because the authorities insisted on hearing his version of the kidnapping. They took a dim view of his nipping back to San Stefano, as he might have known they would! Well—you know his parsimonious habits—he was staying in some fleapit of a hotel, down a backstreet, and he came down with dengue fever.

'Fortunately, Brian was keeping an eye on him, tracked him down and had him treated by the company doctor, who insisted on flying him back to England for further treatment and a complete rest.'

'I knew it would happen,' Claire fretted. 'The way he worked, non-stop, taking it out of himself, it was only a matter of time before he succumbed to some disease or other. Where is he now?'

'I'm not supposed to tell you.' She sensed his smile. 'He's in a hospital in the London area, from which he will be discharged shortly, with strict instructions to convalesce before going back to Rio Negro.'

Claire was deeply sceptical. 'A lot of notice he'll take of those orders. He's going to kill himself, Greg!'

'There's nothing you can do, Claire.' His voice was gentle. 'I know it's hard, if you love him, and you obviously do, but I can't see any way you can prevent him from taking the path he has chosen.'

Prevent him, Claire thought as she put down the phone. No, she could not do that. Nor would she really want to, knowing how committed he was, and how much it meant to him. Love did not consist of standing in the way of the loved one's plans and dreams, or in twisting and changing that person to suit one's requirements. That was the mistake Lisa had made. But neither did it consist of waiting idly on the sidelines for the worst to happen, because of hurt pride and feelings of rejection. That was the mistake *she* had almost made, but it was not too late to rectify it.

Claire paid her hotel bill, checked out, and drove purposefully back to London. Greg had not told her the name of the hospital where Ashley was a patient, but he must have realised when he dropped her the hint that she had a thousand and one contacts in the medical world who would help her find him. Without actually betraying Ashley's entire confidence, he had told her enough to set her on the right track.

It took her an hour on the phone to trace him to St Clement's hospital in Surrey, which employed a well-known specialist in tropical diseases. Dr Wade was still there, her informant told her, but he was due to be discharged tomorrow.

Until that moment she had moved and acted with swift, businesslike efficiency, but now she dithered briefly over what to wear. Did it matter? she asked herself angrily, glaring into her wardrobe. He'd seen her scruffy, sun-burned, and insect-bitten, haggard and dusty, dripping wet and wrapped in a towel . . . was he going to care a jot how she looked, anyway?

It mattered. Claire washed her hair and brushed it until it shone, and carefully selected a black and white striped summer suit she had brought before going away in a vain effort to lift her spirits. She hadn't actually worn it yet, so it needed only a quick press to remove the creases.

She surveyed the girl in the mirror with a sudden rush of doubt. The offer she was about to make to Ashley did not depend on her looking good—in fact, it might be a hindrance. Never mind—her morale needed it. The very audacity of her intentions would falter without a powerful injection of confidence.

St Clement's was set in pleasant surroundings overlooking the playing fields of a nearby school. She had checked the visiting times before setting off, and arrived with plenty of time to spare. But her hands were shaking as she drove into the car park and switched off the engine, and she sat for a full five minutes, summoning up the nerve to go inside. This man does not want to see you, she reminded herself. Have you no self-respect? What you are doing is sheer, unadulterated lunacy.

What I'm doing is the only thing I can do, under the circumstances, she argued back soberly. I love him, and won't let him drive himself to an early grave—not without a struggle. Should I respect myself if I did?

Without further hesitation she got out, slamming the car door and locking it. She knew which ward he was on, and made her way quickly to the Sister's office.

The Sister was young and sprightly, and smiled pleasantly, if a little curiously, at Claire.

'Dr Wade?' she said. 'Yes, he's leaving us tomorrow, to the disappointment of my nurses, who seem to enjoy being alternately teased and insulted. Goodness, but he's a hard man to keep down! He's in the day-room right now, since he hasn't any visitors at the moment. Pop along and see him, if you like—it's just at the end of the corridor.'

Claire smiled and thanked her. Her life seemed to condense to these few moments as she walked down the corridor. The past ceased to exist, the future she hardly dared imagine. Only the next half-hour, and the man she had come here to find, had any relevance. She opened the door nervously.

The day-room was warm and sunny, with windows opening on to a long terrace from which the adjoining playing fields could be seen. The boys from the school were involved in a cricket match—white flannels, the thwack of leather on willow, all so quintessentially English and traditional. And there was Ashley, over by the windows with his back to her, watching the match. Alone, since everyone else was with their visitors.

He must have heard the tap of her heels on the parquet floor as she approached, for he turned his head slightly to see who had entered the room. If he were surprised to discover it was Claire—and he surely must have been— he did not show it.

'Well, Claire,' he said, looking at her soberly, his expression revealing neither pleasure nor anger, 'trust old Greg to open his mouth!'

'You can't blame Greg,' she said, when she could finally risk speaking to him. 'I pestered him unmercifully when I heard about the coup in Rio Negro, until he had to tell me you were in England, and why. The rest I found out for myself.'

He turned back to his apparently absorbing study of the cricket match.

'So you found out. And you're here. What's the point?' he asked distantly.

It took a lot of courage, in view of his seeming lack of enthusiasm, to cross the room until she was standing by his side. Now she could see how much weight had dropped from the already lean frame beneath the pyjamas and dressing-gown, she had to fight hard not to reach up and touch the firmly set line of his jaw, to reassure herself that he was still warm and alive. But she thought it would serve no purpose to dissolve in sentimental tears, and such an overt display of emotion might only embarrass him. So she took a deep breath, and spoke calmly and dispassionately.

'You're a fool, Ashley. If Brian Lawson hadn't decided to keep tabs on you, you'd probably have died in that dump of an hotel where you caught the fever. And where, then, would have been all your fine ideals? Who would have fought the battle of San Stefano in your place? You may be a good doctor, but you aren't Superman!'

'Tell me something I don't already know, Claire.' His voice was distant, verging on boredom. He watched one of the boys at the crease hoist a spanking six, way over the boundary, and clapped politely. 'Oh, well played, lad!'

Claire found that she was talking to the back of his dark head, and a familiar mixture of fury and affection boiled inside her. She wanted to shake him. She wanted to slip her arms around his waist and lean her head on his shoulder. Above all, she had this deep need to do something physical, and it was hard to win this battle with words, with reason and logic.

'You need help out there, in San Stefano,' she said. 'All right, so you can't afford to pay anyone a salary, but two can live almost as cheaply as one, and I have some money saved. I can pay my way. I'm not a nurse, but there are lots of things I can already do, and plenty more I can learn. I know a little Spanish, and can soon pick up more. And without putting Pilar out of a job, I can make your household as well as your practice run more efficiently. In other words, I'm offering you my services as housekeeper, assistant, auxiliary nurse—whatever. I don't see how you can afford to turn me down.'

She was speaking very fast, to prevent any danger of interruption before she had finished what she intended to say. But before she could go any further he spun round, disregarding the match he had been watching with such deep interest minutes ago. His eyes blazed fire, his mouth was tight, and his hands clenched as he faced her—the old, angry, obstreperous Ashley she remembered only too well, but now his wrath had an extra dimension she did not recognise. There was raw pain in the furious blue eyes, and a fierce frustration in the words he wrenched out, with great effort.

'Damn you, Claire, why don't you just go away, and leave me alone?' he cried exasperatedly. 'You don't give up, do you? And I can't take any more! After all I had to go through to send you away from me, here you are, making me suffer it all over again! Give a man a break, won't you?'

She stared at him with the shock of one whose face has been dashed with icy water.

'All you had to go through?' she repeated. 'I tried to stay, but you couldn't wait to get rid of me! You only tolerated my presence because I reminded you of your precious Lisa!'

She wallowed hard, her hands reached out blindly, and, as if magnetised, his caught them and held them painfully tight. She was in his arms, drowning as his mouth found hers, submerging herself in him totally, tears ruining the make-up she had so carefully applied a short time before. When their lips finally broke contact, he still held her, looking down raptly into her face.

'I can't pretend any more, after that!' he said, ruefully. 'Claire, my sweet, you don't know how hard it was to let you leave me. The worst thing, in between bouts of delirium in that ghastly hotel, was thinking that I'd die without seeing your face again—and knowing that if I lived, I still wouldn't see it!'

He fished in the pocket of his dressing-gown, pulled out his wallet, and withdrew a small colour photograph. 'This, for your information, is Lisa,' he said simply.

Claire looked down at the picture of a pretty girl with green eyes and a mass of curly, chestnut hair framing a heart-shaped face.

'But she's not a bit like me!' she gasped.

'Of course she isn't, you ninny!' he said impatiently. 'I told you that to make you think ... well, exactly what you did think, that I was still hankering after her, and fancied you because of the resemblance. But there is no resemblance, either physically or in any other way.'

While Claire still floundered, he summoned up a grin.

'She was here yesterday—some friend who nurses here had phoned her and told her about me, and she came over, all smiles, ready to pick things up where we'd left off. Had I got over all this nonsense, now, and was I ready to settle down and lead a proper life? And oh, it just so happened, there was a residency going at her hospital!'

His free arm tightened around Claire's waist.

'What did you tell her?' she asked tremulously, still only half able to believe what she had heard.

'I told her it wouldn't work, because I was in love with someone else ... which is the truth,' he said. 'All that rubbish I spun you in San Stefano was a decoy. I knew we were in danger of falling for each other, and I couldn't let it happen.'

'Because it was inconvenient, and you didn't have room for a woman in your life?' she asked.

'No, you idiot!' he exclaimed. 'Because I knew I shouldn't set my sights on a woman who already belonged to someone else, and seduce you away from him. Even when I sensed you were beginning to care for me, too. It wasn't right, Claire. It still isn't, I don't operate that way. I feel very bad about it.'

'You mustn't, because it isn't true. It never was,' she told him forcefully. 'Jon and I were finished before I left England, and I don't think I ever loved him, anyway. Making out we were still together began as a convenient fiction to prevent anyone from trying to get too close to me, and as time went on, it grew harder and harder to admit that I'd made it up. It salved my pride a little when I thought you didn't care.'

'Didn't care?' he expostulated. 'I was half out of my mind wanting you! Damn it, woman, I'm not supposed to be subjected to too much stress, right now! I cared too much to condemn a beautiful woman like you, with a flourishing career, to drop everything and live with me in poverty!'

Outside, someone gave a rousing shout of 'Howzat!' and the hitter of sixes marched philosophically back to the pavilion. Claire slid both her hands up Ashley's chest, and rested the palms on his shoulders, looking up at him with a speculative smile.

'Do you love me, Dr Wade?'

'You know it, Ms Mallory,' he replied steadily.

'Man, I reckon that clinches it, as Basil would have put it,' she said. 'You're not going back to San Stefano without me, whatever you say, because I *want* to be there, and I want to be with you—both. And don't spin me those rubbishy hard-luck stories about hard work and poverty, because you don't put off a determined woman so easily.'

She placed a finger against his lips.

'So what do you say? Nicely, mind you. No bad language.'

He bit her finger playfully before answering.

'I *was* taught my manners once, you know, contrary to what you believe, and since we can't possibly live in San Stefano together without benefit of clergy, I'll ask you *nicely* to be my wife. Only once. You don't get asked twice, so if you're going to say yes, make it snappy.' He gathered her close to him again, murmured in her ear, 'The Yorkshire Dales are quite pleasant at this time of year. Still cool enough to make a warm bed a good place to be at night!'

'You could wait until I give my consent,' she smiled.

'You have, lass. Oh, but you have,' he told her, and now the players on the field were performing to a gallery who could not have cared less for their talents. The couple in the day-room did not hear the bell signifying that visiting was over, or notice Sister standing in the doorway with a bemused expression on her face.

Well, really! Only yesterday, Dr Wade had sent one girl running out in tears because of some caustic remark, and now here he was, locked in a passionate embrace with another... you just never could tell!

Greg missed the wedding because he was on his way back from a full board meeting of General Chemicals in New York, but he hot-footed it off Concorde in time to give the newly-weds the good tidings, just as they were about to set off on their honeymoon.

'Couldn't have gone better,' he enthused warmly. 'The company is not only going to back you to the hilt, but they're starting a medical foundation to set up health centres in remote, backward parts of the world. Ashley, you're invited to be one of the directors, so when you've got San Stefano working properly, you can train someone to take over while you move on to start up the next.'

The bridegroom looked pleased, startled, and doubtful by turn.

'That's terrific—more than I could have hoped for when I first wrote to you,' he said. 'But ... a director? Do you ever think I'll make a good bureaucrat?'

'Hopeless,' Greg said, and they all laughed. 'We want you to be medical director, and you can go right on organising that end of things, only with more money, more power, more influence to do good. And you'll have Claire to help you. Now, *she'll* make an excellent bureaucrat!'

Claire slung a handful of confetti at him in retaliation, and Basil, who was taking the photographs, snapped them gleefully as they got into the car.

'Right now,' said Ashley, looking into the eyes of his new bride, 'this medical director is strictly off duty. So come along, Ms Mallory—sorry, I mean *Mrs* Wade. From now on, you're in charge of my convalescence.'

'Only the convalescence?' she murmured with a smile. 'What about the rest of your life?'

'We'll sort that one out when we come to it, lass,' Ashley promised, and put the car in gear.

BETRAYALS. DECISIONS AND CHOICES. . .

BUY OUT by David Wind   £2.95

The money-making trend of redeveloping Manhattan tenement blocks sets the scene for this explosive novel. In the face of shady deals and corrupt landlords, tenants of the Crestfield begin a fight for their rights – and end up in a fight for their lives.

BEGINNINGS by Judith Duncan   £2.50

Judith Duncan, bestselling author of "Into the Light", blends sensitivity and insight in this novel of a woman determined to make a new beginning for herself and her children. But an unforeseen problem arises with the arrival of Grady O'Neil.

ROOM FOR ONE MORE by Virginia Nielsen   £2.75

At 38, Charlotte Emlyn was about to marry Brock Morley – 5 years her junior. Then her teenage son announced that his girlfriend was pregnant. Could Brock face being husband, stepfather *and* grandfather at 33? Suddenly 5 years seemed like a lifetime – but could the dilemma be overcome?.

**These three new titles will be out in bookshops from
MAY 1989**

W☉RLDWIDE

*Available from Boots, Martins, John Menzies, W.H. Smith, Woolworths
and other paperback stockists.*

ROMANCE

Next month's romances from Mills & Boon

Each month, you can choose from a world of variety in romance with Mills & Boon. These are the new titles to look out for next month.

TOUCH THE FLAME Helen Bianchin
RING OF GOLD Sandra Field
A REASON FOR BEING Penny Jordan
RIDDELL OF RIVERMOON Miriam Macgregor
NIGHT WITH A STRANGER Joanna Mansell
EYE OF THE STORM Sandra Marton
CONFLICT Margaret Mayo
NO NEED TO SAY GOODBYE Betty Neels
A MATTER OF FEELING Sophie Weston
THE MAXTON BEQUEST Alison York
BELONGING Sally Cook
ISLAND DECEPTION Elizabeth Duke
WHEN WE'RE ALONE Jane Donnelly
FOOLISH DECEIVER Sandra K. Rhoades

Buy them from your usual paperback stockist, or write to: Mills & Boon Reader Service, P.O. Box 236, Thornton Rd, Croydon, Surrey CR9 3RU, England. Readers in Southern Africa — write to: Independent Book Services Pty, Postbag X3010, Randburg, 2125, S. Africa.

Mills & Boon
the rose of romance

AROUND THE WORLD WORDSEARCH
COMPETITION!

How would you like a years supply of Mills & Boon Romances ABSOLUTELY FREE? Well, you can win them! All you have to do is complete the word puzzle below and send it in to us by October 31st. 1989. The first 5 correct entries picked out of the bag after that date will win **a years supply of Mills & Boon Romances** (*ten books every month - worth around £150*) What could be easier?

R	D	N	A	L	R	E	Z	T	I	W	S
E	O	N	M	C	H	I	N	A	A	C	C
G	M	U	I	G	L	E	B	N	N	U	O
Y	E	C	E	G	W	H	I	Z	C	B	T
P	D	R	H	S	E	R	I	A	Z	A	L
T	N	S	M	P	E	R	U	N	D	D	A
N	A	W	I	A	T	P	I	I	E	N	N
Y	L	A	T	I	N	A	N	A	N	A	D
N	G	S	T	N	H	Y	D	E	M	L	Q
W	N	O	J	A	M	A	I	C	A	L	A
R	E	L	A	D	A	N	A	C	R	O	R
T	H	A	I	L	A	N	D	D	K	H	I

ITALY	THAILAND	SCOTLAND	SWITZERLAND
GERMANY	IRAQ	JAMAICA	
HOLLAND	ZAIRE	TANZANIA	
BELGIUM	TAIWAN	PERU	
EGYPT	CANADA	SPAIN	
CHINA	INDIA	DENMARK	
NIGERIA	ENGLAND	CUBA	

PLEASE TURN OVER FOR DETAILS ON HOW TO ENTER

HOW TO ENTER

All the words listed overleaf, below the word puzzle, are hidden in the grid. You can find them by reading the letters forward, backwards, up or down, or diagonally. When you find a word, circle it or put a line through it, the remaining letters (which you can read from left to right, from the top of the puzzle through to the bottom) will spell a secret message.

After you have filled in all the words, don't forget to fill in your name and address in the space provided and pop this page in an envelope (you don't need a stamp) and post it today. Hurry - competition ends October 31st. 1989.

Mills & Boon Competition,
FREEPOST,
P.O. Box 236,
Croydon,
Surrey. CR9 9EL
Only one entry per household

Secret Message _____

_____

Name _____

Address _____

_____

_____

_____ Postcode _____

You may be mailed as a result of entering this competition

COMP 6